CHILD
of the
BLACK SUN

ADAM CRAIG

Published by Liquorice Fish Books
an imprint of Cinnamon Press,
Office 49019, PO Box 15113, Birmingham, B2 2NJ
www.cinnamonpress.com

The right of Adam Craig to be identified as author of this work has been asserted by him in accordance with the Copyright, Designs and Patent Act, 1988. © 2022 Adam Craig.

Print Edition ISBN 978-1-911540-18-2
Ebook Edition ISBN 978-1-911540-19-9

British Library Cataloguing in Publication Data. A CIP record for this book can be obtained from the British Library.

All rights reserved. No part of this publication may be reproduced, stored in a retrieval system, or transmitted in any form or by any means, electronic, mechanical, photocopying, recording or otherwise without the prior written permission of the publishers. This book may not be lent, hired out, resold or otherwise disposed of by way of trade in any form of binding or cover other than that in which it is published, without the prior consent of the publishers.

Cover and interior designed and typeset by Adam Craig/Liquorice Fish Books.

Liquorice Fish Books is represented by Inpress.

to Ming, who believed enough for both of us;

to Jan, who always knows where soul is strongest;

and

Seth, for not giving up.

PRAGUE

IN THE WEEKS after she left, the light drained from the world and each colour took on a leaden cast. His friend Karel told him she was just a girl. And there are girls everywhere, Karel added, waving a hand towards the people hurrying to and fro, to and fro. But, Honza argued, tracing a finger around the interlocked ring-stains on the tabletop, but Karel had loved her, written poems to her, he must care, he must— Karel laughed and pointed to a young woman outside, or that one over there, what did it matter? Honza startled, searched each face passing the café window. Just in case.

But she was gone.

Jaromír, the photographer, asked Honza to help construct a series of images. *Modernist abstractions in light*, was how Jaromír described them, asking for Honza's help again and again until relenting seemed easier than not. Jaromír talked theory and light and form as they moved sheets of glass and objects, selected almost at random, around the studio. Strong sunlight waned, waxed through the tall windows. Shadows flexed out of each shape, camera positioned to see only shadow, shadow and refracted light, each material object attenuated, only essence remaining. Or essence lost.

Honza looked up, sure the studio itself was no longer solid, surfaces uncertain and suggesting something lay beneath. Something hidden in the next instant, long before there was chance to understand, or know if he had glimpsed anything at all.

'And you?'

The waiter had taken their order and left two glass tankards of dark beer.

Nothing more ordinary than a tavern, nothing more concrete.

Jaromír took a sip of beer and tried again: 'How's your work coming along?'

But Honza had not drawn a line nor wanted to paint in weeks. Not since she had left without warning, without a proper goodbye. *Forgive me*, her note had read.

> *Forgive me. Have to go. A friend is showing the*
> *way and I must leave at once.*
> *Marietta*

Staring at each word, certain they must have another meaning, that he was seeing them wrongly, that if he read them again and again then—

Her note kept saying the same thing, even when he had run all the way to Karel's apartment, breathless and babbling, Karel shrugging and laughing, Honza confused, doubting the words he used meant what they seemed to. But Karel had no idea where she was. It made no sense and Honza left, Karel calling after him as he ran down the stairs, ran back to his own studio to line up each canvas, a dozen of them (*Why do you want to paint me?*) more than a dozen (*You're beautiful*) each one of her (*Me? No*) each placed in the order he had painted them. Kneeling (*Yes*) Honza searched them for an explanation (*Inside as much as outside more so*) back and forth (*Your beauty grows the deeper I look*) back and forth (*but it's elusive in paint on canvas elusive so that's*). Nothing made sense.

Forgive me

Night came and knelt with him in front of the paintings, a moon, no longer full, peered through the garret windows, its light passing over the gestures his hands had made, each recorded in paint and pigment, moonlight whispering and Honza beginning to nod (*That's why I have to paint you keep painting*) to think he—

But it was nonsense, he yelled at himself, at the paintings of her (*Marietta!*), snatching up a knife, slashing and cutting at cold canvas and long-dried paint, each empty of meaning. Just shapes, (*You're beautiful and special*) he sobbed, hurling each ragged frame at the walls until there were only splinters and his breath came in shudders, tears burning against his cheeks as (*I have to paint because*) the last of the rage left and he collapsed. The night and the moon knelt beside him and, gradually, something came to hover in the silvered darkness.

Or so it had seemed, he had reminded himself next morning as grief finished hollowing out his heart, all colour and desire turning bitter and thin.

'Do you dream?'

Marie had suggested he come along. It was a 'salon' she had said, not a party, a group of writers and artists driven to the search for the wondrous in the apparently mundane. He had not liked the sound of it. She had insisted. So he stood in a corner and hoped to be ignored.

'Of course you do,' the woman interrupted before he had chance to reply. 'Everyone does, you know.' Her accent was clipped and precise. Honza had thought she must be British aristocracy. She had cleaved a line through the guests at the salon and introduced herself to him: 'My name is Imogen, Imogen Carwithen. You're an artist, aren't you?' And she had told him she was Irish, not British, although she had been born on the other side of the world. 'A Celt at heart, you see,' Imogen had explained before fixing an intense gaze on him and asking about his dreams.

'Everyone dreams but they rarely remember their dreams, so the question is: do you remember yours?'

He shook his head and looked for an escape.

'What do you remember?' Imogen place a hand lightly on his arm and each excuse and outright insult evaporated before he could voice them.

'A man,' he admitted. 'An old man.' Determined that was enough, Honza would have said no more but something in her silence prompted him to add: 'Sometimes he's pointing. I think he's telling me to stay away. Like the other man does.'

'Other man?'

'Yes.' He glanced around the room. Wanting a drink or wanting to leave, unsure which. Imogen's hand did not leave his arm.

'What colour is this other man's hair?'

'Dark. Black. Dark—'

'And the sun?'

'There is no sun. Please, I must—'

'Its colour?'

'No colour, no sun, no— Would you please—'

'And the woman?' Imogen insisted, voice low and urgent as her gaze refused to let him move. 'What about the woman?'

'Please, she— she—'

'Oh, Im, don't bother the fellow so. Can't you see he's desperate for a drink?'

Tall. Ash-blond hair offset by eyes ice-blue, crystalline and penetrating, unreadable themselves, face oval about a mouth that might be refined, or louche, or cruel, or urbane, in moments or consecutively, smile a mask through which the eyes observed. All.

Honza looked away.

'Godfrey,' Imogen sighed, her hand slipping from Honza's arm. 'Your capacity for ill-manners and untimely interruption—'

'Oh hush, Imogen, do hush. You're Pernath, aren't you? Honza Pernath?' Eyes of ice-blue, gaze steady, unblinking. Until Honza nodded and Godfrey smiled. 'Ah, capital. I saw your work here, in '35, and again in Paris earlier this year. It has great merit.'

'High praise,' Imogen explained, her expression unreadable.

Honza searched for a reply. 'Do you paint, Mister…?'

'Not a bit.' Godfrey drained his glass and snorted. 'I collect. Amongst other things.'

'You're being deliberately mysterious, Godfrey.' Imogen offered them a brittle smile, the tall man ignoring her completely and presenting Honza with a visiting card.

Godfrey A. Howden
Bloomsbury
& Tremadog

'If you ever come to Albion, dear chap, do look me up.' Godfrey looped his arm through Imogen's. 'Call the London number. And consider this a standing invitation, Herr Pernath. Anytime, anytime.' Godfrey Howden turned, expecting Imogen to follow his lead. She slipped free of his arm, leaning close to Honza, her whisper almost lost in the hubbub of laughter and voices raised in debate and discussion. She stood back, letting Howden tug on her arm, offering a hearty goodnight as they vanished into the throng.

There was a sun.

It hung over the waves, fatter than any noonday sun, face dark and cankerous. Despite its weight, bending the clouds and twisting the distant horizon out of true, the sea remained motionless beneath the black sun, caught between swells, each wavecrest edged in shimmering jet, all highlights turned to negative, every shadow threatening to turn itself inside out.

A breeze maundered, turning circles as it skimmed over the dunes, shying from the tideline to stumble inland, mumbling the same few words, the same few words setting the grass to hiss, words swallowed by the rustle of marram and sand, grain against grain, and yet just out of reach, almost on the edge of understanding, almost…

Honza took a step towards dunes and found himself facing the black sun, not fearful but sure it was towards the dunes he should be walking. And his next step, which should have brought him further up the beach, instead took him towards the black sun, its mouldering face a veil that suggested something hidden beneath.

Better to turn back than look closer. Yet behind him his prints in the sand made an uneven line towards the unmoving breakers, the sun fixed above them. And ahead across sand otherwise unmarred more footprints leading him forwards, marks not entirely solid, not yet made, needing him to take the next step to bring each into being. Honza resisted, felt terror crawl up his back and plant itself around his throat—

He was a shape scoured from foam and fleck, thrashing the nearest waves into frenzy, alarm slapping Honza across the face, stiff-arming him back a step as—another lurch— the man threw off the sea with a scything of his arms that became a run, man's feet kicking up sand, sand scattering, obliterating each footprint yet to be made, Honza's path broken.

As the sand fell, so did Honza, the man from the sea already halfway to the dunes by the time he managed to sit up, man's arms windmilling, a frenzy that fought the breeze, the salt-spiced air, hands protecting the man's downturned face. Face hidden. Only his hair certain: dark, dark as the sun overhead.

The man's anxiety was infectious. Honza dragged himself to his feet and followed, own arms churning, desperation urging more speed, more haste, more space between him and the shore, more space between him and the black sun above.

In the moment before he plunged into the dunes— dark-haired man already somewhere in their shifting, whispering maze—there might have been someone else on the beach. Waving. To encourage him to run faster. Surely that. Surely that's what the old man wanted him to do.

Honza ran. Faster. Fell against a dune. Tripped. Over marram. Staggered. Kept. On. Running. Black sun a pressure between his shoulders, daring him to look, turn back, look…

Pushing further inland, each step harder than the last, sand soft growing softer until he had to slow, pace slackened in a single step, dune crests mounting one on the next all around, as far as he could see. Further.

The wind held its peace.

The grass stood. Watching.

He turned.

A shape appeared in the distance, indistinct against the grey of cloud, scaling the dunes to climb into the sky. So distant it might have been the old man, or the dark-haired man from the sea.

Honza pressed a hand to his mouth, afraid of sound or breath.

But she was already gone, down beneath the crest of the dune, gone into the blackness that swallowed sand and beach and sea and left him alone with the jet-dark sun. Until, with a yell, Honza managed to wake up.

There was a black sun. Just as she had said. He tried not to think of how she could have known.

Marie suggested he go to Paris.

Half the sky was filled with bruised cloud, sun holding court over the balance, a monarch golden and far too brilliant to gaze at, so the only direction to look out of the tavern window was towards the cloud, dour and slate-hard.

Honza took a gulp of beer.

'You've been there, they know you. And I can make more introductions, dealers…' She trailed into silence.

A speck of rain kissed the window, sunlight appearing brighter as the clouds grew darker.

'Can't paint.' Honza drained his glass (*Don't you get tired of painting me?*) signalled for another.

'A change of place, it might get you out of this—' Marie paused, picked up again as if she had always meant to say: 'might inspire you.' She drained her glass of wine and asked the barman for another as he sloshed a fresh tankard of beer in front of Honza.

More rain pressed against the window. Sun no less brilliant.

'Change of place?' Honza took a mouthful of beer and dismissed the notion. 'Wouldn't make a difference.' Each time he blinked, her face appeared (*I couldn't get bored with painting you never never because I*) an after-image hanging between him and the window, rain peppering her careworn face, a face that might have been dismissed as plain but which he could never look away from, never tire of what he saw there and in her eyes.

(*Tell me, Honza, what do you know of*)

'What do you know of alchemy?' He pushed the glass tankard back a little, fingertip marking patterns in the spilled beer.

'Lead into gold, same as anyone.' Marie sipped her wine. 'Except some say it's about the spirit. Or the soul. Not metals, anyway.'

'There's a difference? Spirit and soul?'

(*Yes*)

Marie had no idea. 'But the point is to make the psyche more balanced, less leaden, more... pure, I suppose. Why?'

Honza picked up his beer. 'No reason.'

He put down the tankard without taking a sip.

'What does "the star in the sea" mean?' Or "star from the sea"?' Neither meant anything to Marie. Reluctantly, he admitted it had come to him in a dream. Marie was fascinated, wanting to know more, wanting him to write it all down and present it to the next meeting of her surrealist group. Honza repeated that the phrase was all he could remember, there was nothing to write down and less to report, searching until he found a change of subject.

As the rain beat heavily against the windows, he

remembered the wind through the marram grass, its sibilant whispers always on the edge of comprehension, with him when he woke.

The star from the sea.

Licking its fingers, the rain snuffed out the sun and drew an early twilight over the city.

Marie had tried again to persuade him to go to Paris. She would be exhibiting there herself soon and she and her husband would be staying for several months, what better chance…

Perhaps it was the beer, loosening his temper and making resentment leak into his heart so it beat faster, bringing a flush to his face as it clipped his voice. Honza struggled not to tell her to stop meddling, to understand he was no longer a painter, that part of his life closed and lost…

When they stepped into the rain, Marie asked him to think about it and Honza managed to swallow his rage long enough to say he might, to thank her for being such a good friend.

Only when the downpour had washed her reflection from the pavement did he curse and yell, tears bringing salt to the rain.

The twilight hooded the faces of the saints lining the bridge, bowed heads watching people hurrying by, or turned away in contemplation, or sorrow. Honza slumped against the parapet, the waters of the Vltava almost hidden in the gloom, lights coming on around the castle on the hill. An old legend had it that Lucifer had plummeted to earth at the place where the castle now stood, the castle mount thrown up by the impact. Honza blinked rain from his eyes, wondered what it would be like to fall so far, crash so hard to earth.

Someone laughed. He looked around.

A couple, arm-in-arm, sheltering under an umbrella. The woman laughed again. A newspaper vendor called out the afternoon headlines. A flare of light, a man's face suggested by a match flame, cigarette smoke billowing. Honza pressed a hand across his face, pushing away the smell. Weeks since he his last smoke, not since… not since…

The rain soaked him. No overcoat, water leaking down his neck, his shoes. Too cold to be angry. Only miserable.

He peered at the statue beside him. The saint pretended not to notice, staring into mid-distance, dingy halo dripping. Honza searched out the statue's eyes, newspaper vendor's voice fading, splash and tramp of pedestrians forgotten as he tried to make eye contact. Shadows masked part of the saint's face, face unfamiliar although Honza had walked along the bridge countless times, had made studies of every statue and knew them all by name. All but this one. And that could not be so. Honza shaded his eyes from the rain, looked closer.

The saint's gaze flickered until it settled on Honza.

The rain made no sound, the Vltava likewise hushed.

Honza could not look away, the bronze gaze so intent, the halo bleeding darkness into the twilight. The city stole off, soundless shadow gone to leave them on the bridge, bridge leading nowhere, neither here nor there, bronze no longer inflexible if not quite flesh, saint stretching out a hand, fingers curled around something hidden. Better to look away, some part of him advised, better not to be involved, he had enough to worry about, but Honza could not move. Could only watch the fingers unfurl, a single word lying in the saint's palm, word an apparition revealed so that Honza saw the word and heard the word in his mind, or elsewhere, the word whispering itself to him. Whispering:

astrum

A hand grabbed his shoulder.

'Don't throw yourself in, old boy, it's not worth it.'

Noise, bustle, the Vltava reciting lists of the hundreds of places it must visit, rain petered almost to a stop. The clouds had grown thin and a little of real dusk painted the rooftops with the last of the day's sun.

'Whatever's wrong with you?'

The nearest statues were metres away on either side, this place along the parapet roughly halfway between.

'Still moping then?'

'Hm?' He focused: young man, young woman clinging to his arm. Searching for the umbrella. But this was not the couple he had seen earlier. 'Karel?'

'Snap out of this, old boy, life's too short.' Karel wormed his arm around his girlfriend's waist, squeezing hard, a giggle bursting from her.

Karel had told him how lucky he was because she had clearly preferred Honza. Lucky swine Karel had said and made another attempt to lure her away, declaring he couldn't sleep for thinking of her, couldn't think without speaking of her.

(*Marietta*)

Marietta.

Karel gave him a light punch on the arm. 'Seriously, look at the state of you. Is it worth it?'

'Karel?'

His friend pushed his face close, breath thick with the ash of cigarettes, last drags of a bottle of cheap brandy. 'It's not worth it, old boy. You've got to live.'

The young woman giggled.

'But—' Honza lost track of the first words that came to mind. 'But… you loved her.'

'Your plain girl?' Karel laughed. 'Don't start again, Honza.' Karel kissed his girlfriend. 'I might have done, for a few days. Why not? You have to try, don't you? But it's not worth all this, Honza, it's not worth all this, not in the end it's not. She's gone, Honza, so what? Find someone better. Like I have.'

Karel kissed his girlfriend again and she giggled.

Honza did not move. Did not speak. Throat locked, it was hard to breathe, shaking so badly he could only watch as

Karel waved and the pair sauntered away. Watching long after they had gone from view, rage doing nothing to stop the cold seeping deep into his bones, the last of the afternoon light gritty and the city's clamour painfully loud.

In the first moments: a room, clothes strewn across a chair, a shirt choking the light from a lamp, big windows, night, sink piled, plates— Pieces, taken at a glance, struggling to wake, to understand this place, name it. Pounding, thumping, hands beating against a door, calling a name.
'Honza! Honza!'
Throwing off sleep with the blankets, garret slewing into focus as he rolled out of bed. Familiar again—
'Honza! In the name of anything you hold to be holy, open this bloody door, why don't you!'
—the hammering not familiar.
'Unless you're fucking!' shouted another voice.
'Even if you are!' called a third. 'Open up, we know you're in there.' A kick landed on the door. More hammering. 'Just open!'
'Open!' chimed in the chorus.
He threw open the door. 'What the bloody hell do you—'
They tackled him, two grabbing him around the waist, third gathering flailing legs. Laughing as they carted him across the garret and dropped him on the bed.
A pair of trousers hit him in the face.
'Dress, dress, dress.' One of them began to clap in time to the chant. Another took his shoulders. Trousers snatched away and one of his feet forced into them.
'Let go,' Honza protested. His assailants had other ideas, trousers hoisted as they dragged him vertical. A shirt half-threaded over one arm. Other arm thrust into a jacket. One shoe stuffed into its pocket as he was lifted, struggling and swearing, to have the other jammed onto a foot. Door slamming behind them. Honza almost falling. Don't dawdle,

they ordered, don't think, act, act and be spontaneous.

Cold night air.

Flagstones eager to chill his unshod foot.

They said nothing about where they were taking him. Only pointed. A figure waited at the corner under a street lamp. Hat low and trench coat collar pulled up.

Honza pressed a hand to his mouth, afraid of sound, of breath.

A hand materialised from the trench coat pocket. Not a pistol to go with the gangster's sharp clothes. A match, scraped against the lamp post, flame evicting shadows from under the hat brim. Revealing Marie's face.

She smiled. 'Do you like?'

'Dashing.'

'Oh.' She lit her cigarette, American, of course, to go with the outfit. 'I was hoping for hard-boiled, like in the movies.' Marie offered him a cigarette. Honza shook his head.

'I'd rather go back to bed,' he said, hopping to slip on the second shoe before handing Marie his jacket and adjusting his clothes. He must have slept the clock round since seeing Karel on the Charles Bridge, since... standing beside the saint. Slept the clock round and more. 'I don't want to do this, whatever it is, Marie.'

The three kidnappers wailed and jeered. Honza ignored them. 'Thanks, but...'

Marie's expression wavered. She sniffed, drew hard on the cigarette and squared her shoulders. 'No. It's time you got out, did something ridiculous. Something marvellous.' She took his arm and tugged.

They called it an 'expedition'. A large group of the surrealists and their friends, wandering through the heart of the city, taking turns whenever they glimpsed something that caught their imagination, treating the familiar as alien, searching for encounters with the unexpected. The wondrous.

Honza remembered Marietta talking of such things.

He had never quite understood what she meant, although her yearning was clear. He tramped behind Marie and the others as they exclaimed and pointed and made grandiose speculations, mired in his own thoughts.

The streets of the old town roved and branched around them. Autumn loitered in the shadows between the pools of lamp-light. It breathed on windows and drew patterns in the mist. Passers-by little more than shapes, the glow of a cigarette, footsteps reverberating. A motor-car's horn became the whinnying of a horse, itself no more than a snatch of laughter, the ringing of a bell.

A group of puppets in a shop window beckoned the explorers closer and they gathered around, exchanging stories and offering words to be placed in the puppets' mouths. Honza frowned, thinking it better if the puppets were left to speak for themselves. At the centre of the display stood a king and queen, their hands joined in eternal union. The queen ignored him but the king watched sidelong, gaze almost making contact.

'They call this the Royal Way, you know.' Voice close to his ear. Honza concentrated on the king, unwilling to acknowledge the explorer's comment.

'An ancient route through the city,' the voice continued, soft and unconcerned, hardly intruding on his attention. 'Symbolic as well as ritual, linked to the stages of the *opus alchymicum*, the alchemists' Great Work.'

The King's head was inclined, just a little.

On the other side of the throng, Marie made a comment and drew gasps of approval and a round of applause.

The king's expression froze. Only wood and paint.

They moved on. Here a dragon, coiled around a doorway. There a moon hid half its face, inscrutable as the building it decorated.

'It's said,' the voice murmured, 'that no one knows the meaning of these signs on the walls, what the point of all this was.'

A fork in the road waited. Marie announced they must follow the left branch, explorers filing after her. Honza failed to notice, mind circling the king and the queen, hands joined inseparably. Still straggling at the rear, he wandered up the right-hand fork. Silence trailed beside him, the street deserted.

'Oh but friend, you should see this.' The voice murmured close into his ear.

Honza looked up.

'There, above the door...' The voice seemed above him and Honza looked up further.

'Do you see?'

A black sun.

It peered down from the lintel of a heavy wooden door, building set into another parting of the road, neither to the left nor to the right but at the centre of the way, a street lamp tracing a finger across its surface.

'We should go in.'

Black sun not featureless. A full face, fleshy. Something come to ripeness. Or a bit beyond.

'It's...' Expression forbidding. Not stern, nor hostile. But wanting Honza to turn away. 'It's locked, surely.'

'Shall we try?'

Honza shook his head. Yet the handled turned, iron dark and silent.

The door swung open. Light from the streetlamp only reached a little across the threshold, shadows solid after that. Honza glanced up but the black sun's expression was unchanged. 'I can't go in.'

'For a few moments,' the voice murmured, close to his ear so that it was almost like a hand on the shoulder, supporting. 'Only that.'

Darkness made way for his first step, let him make a second, footfalls echoing softly, suggesting space, a vaulted entrance hall, or chamber of some sort.

The light from outside could not follow him any further and after another few heartbeats the door shut with a click.

Darkness drew close and a surge of panic blinded him, its white flare turning into pitch that pooled, brought silence. No thought, only sensation: his breath slowing, air cool against his skin, heart's beat beating, marking moments, winding itself through the abundance-into-famine of the moon's wax and wane, the come and go of days and seasons. He could smell his own sweat, and the musk of grief oily beneath a trace of cigarette smoke lingering on his clothes. All of a piece, as much as the creak and flex of tendon and the dull ache in his feet or in the muscles of shoulder and neck. There to be experienced, in this moment, the moments that followed, each passing into the next so they might have been the same moment, eternal and yet mutable.

Changeless but changing even so, the darkness condensed to tease highlight from nothing and shadow out of blackness, forms unfolding, flexing neck and body, one shaking wings, other catlike in its stretch, jewelled skin glimmering in the unlight filling the room, twin dragons standing close together so they might have been of one body, joined inseparably, one torso burnished, graced with wings that arced as they rose, wrote on the air, the other sleek, wingless, muscles taught beneath scales that glistened, moonlight on quicksilver.

They might have been statues. Next moment, they seemed alive, caught for an instant between stillness and swiftness. Perhaps they were both, Honza thought, thought evaporating as he took a step closer, aware of the room and his body and the presence of the dragons, everything else gone in this instant that flowed unnoticed into each instant passed, each instant still ahead.

The cry raked against silence and dark. Hands jerked him backwards, cry coming again and again. Rage and fear, cry finding its way to Honza's mouth, infecting. He fell to the floor, the dark-haired man stumbling over him, almost falling, flailing at the twin dragons with his fists, beating the air and yelling louder as if even wild misses were blows landed, victories made.

The dragons peered down at the dark-haired man, aloof and unmoved.

Honza began to crawl.

'No.'

The voice rose a second time.

'Please—'

Honza began to run. Hitting the door with his shoulder as he rushed into the street, terror riding his shoulders, driving, driving, dark-haired man's yells running beside him, driving, driving, until there was nothing, not breath nor cobble nor running.

Only blackness.

A nimble breeze picked leaves from branches and threaded them into loose garlands trailed along the gutters or swayed in serpentine dance through the greying air. Honza did not notice.

Sleepless nights. Days in the garret, door latch thrown, breath held whenever the stairs creaked or someone moved along the hallways. Apprehensive in case there was another attempt to drag him out of himself. Honza huddled amongst the empty easels and scraps of canvas, back to the windows, aware only of the dim light draining out of another day or of the night lost in thought, oblivious.

Dragons...

Dark-haired man...

A king...

(*Wondrous*)

A bitter, grizzled morning watched him uncertainly as he burst into the street. Honza hurried, head down and shoulders hunched, unsure his nerve would hold. Costermongers whistled American pop tunes as they unloaded a dray, horse with its nose in a bag of oats and unmoved by 'Begin the Beguine' or 'A-Tisket A-Tasket'. One of the costermongers watched Honza pass, pockmarked features lined and careworn. *Like Marietta.* The thought prompted Honza to meet the man's gaze, costermonger saying something he failed to catch. A lock of the man's hair had escaped his cap. Not black but dark, dark beginning to grey. Honza shifted his gaze, looked back a few steps later but the costermonger was heaving another barrel off the dray as his companion attempted a tune by Benny Goodman.

It was not where he thought it had been. And when he finally found the door, it was little like he remembered from the expedition. Fat faced, the black sun pursed its lips and peered into mid-distance, oblivious to street and passers-by, more the face of a contented burgher than a disapproving critic, the road running directly past moulding and heavily-studded door, not forking around them at all.

Honza studied the face: black sun set within Baroque scrollwork, the wedged beams radiating from it almost Art Deco in style... Vaguely like he remembered, at least. He pulled sketch book and pencils from an inside pocket and began to draw. Studies from different angles, drafting and redrafting the face, sketches from his... experience (Honza could think of no other word for the evening of the expedition) crowding the edges and corners of most of the pages. He knew he had walked this lane before, many times probably. He had to have seen the masque and the door, even if he had no memory of ever giving either more than a glance. A dream, then. A fugue. Or hysteria... He turned over another page, began another study, pencil restless, searching the cream paper for... for...

'Handsome emblem, isn't it?'

Imogen Carwithen nodded a greeting as she came to stand beside him, a sage green Inverness cape offset by a ruby red beret, the scarf in shades of emerald coiled around her neck a tame serpent she might charm into action at any moment.

She smiled.

'Inspiration for a new painting?' She indicated the masque.

'No.' The silence was uncomfortable and he needed to

fill it but had no idea what to say.

'You have another reason, perhaps, for an interest in the Royal Art?' When he looked perplexed, Imogen nodded again towards the black sun. 'Alchemy.'

'I... I had a friend who was interested.'

Imogen raised a carefully plucked eyebrow. The breeze twitched the skirts of her coat. She shooed it away, scrutiny of Honza never wavering. He began to fidget.

'A practitioner, then.' Imogen smiled.

Honza tried to hide his confusion. 'I don't think she ever had a laboratory. She was just interested.'

Imogen held his gaze for a fraction longer than was comfortable. Casually, she rummaged in her shoulder bag and took out a sketchbook of her own, a graphite stick from a tin box and, with deft strokes, transferred the black sun to paper, transmuting stone to charcoal.

'There is more than one way of practicing alchemy,' she told him as she worked. 'As many paths as alchemists, it's said.'

'You're an artist. I thought, the other night, at the salon...'

'I make my living through Art.'

Honza could hear the capital A, although he had no idea what Imogen meant by it. Uncomfortable in her presence, sure he knew less now than he had setting out this morning. The wind pulled at his coat. Perhaps it wanted him to stay. 'I must go.'

'Of course.' Imogen began another study. 'And your dreams? How are they?'

'I, er, I don't recall my dreams.'

'Of course. *Stella a mari*, eh?'

Backing away from her, no breath to speak. Only stagger into a walk that became headlong, blind and headlong, until there was no breath left at all.

Imogen was sitting at the top of the stairs when he finally returned to the garret.

He stepped around her without speaking, unlocking the door and leaving it open as he filled a kettle and set it on the gas ring, shucking his overcoat, a trail of water spats winding across the floor behind him, a pilgrim's way ending at the windows. Rain beat the glass, whistled up by the breeze grown tired of stealing leaves.

'I apologise.' Imogen leaned against the doorframe. 'I didn't intend to scare you.'

'I'm not scared,' Honza snapped, scrubbing a towel over his head before dropping the threadbare rag as he knelt to lay a fire in the grate. 'And how did you bloody well find me?'

The kettle began to whistle.

'I asked Marie.' Imogen turned off the gas and poured a little water into the tea pot, swirling to warm the vessel. 'This one?' She held up a packet of herb tea from the shelf above the gas ring. Honza shrugged, pretending to be preoccupied with setting his shoes to dry and finding dry socks.

Only the wind spoke and in the rain's borrowed voice at that.

Honza held out his hands to the fire. He knew he was being petulant, knew this resentment was as much to do with grief as this woman's strange behaviour. He could not think how to say as much, not without feeling ridiculous. He had never felt this awkward with Marietta. She was so gentle and open, so kind, so…

Wondrous, he thought, eyes prickling and throat growing tight, body turning in on itself as his gut contracted, shoulders hunching around the sorrow of her leaving.

'Please don't let your tea grow cold.' Imogen spoke softly, words a palm against his face, comforting.

He glanced up. She was sitting at the small table, cups and teapot at the centre waiting patiently. As was Imogen. *Take the time you need*: her posture, her expression said this clearly. Honza found more tears, unable to look at Imogen directly as he sat opposite her.

'I'm most terribly sorry for your loss, Honza.' Imogen placed a steaming cup within easy reach and sat back.

'I…' Even this many words were too many. Honza shivered, sipping from the cup. Eventually, he mumbled: 'I thought I'd find her, follow her, you see. But… there are no clues. And I despise myself,' he added with a passion that slopped tea across his hands and the table. 'For not trying harder, not keeping her, not loving her enough to be able to find her…'

Imogen handed him the ragged towel and sat down again. 'There's only so much anyone can do.'

'I know. I know and still…' He scrubbed his face and wadded the towel. 'It's not enough.'

'No. And one must come to live with that knowledge.' Imogen sipped her tea. 'This may be little consolation—and I may be wrong, Honza—but it may be that the path your young woman is travelling is not one you could find, let alone follow, in any event.'

'What do you know?' he demanded. 'Has she been kidnapped? Is she dead? What?' He lunged and gripped Imogen's arm, tea cup overturning across the tabletop. 'What?'

'I'm sorry but I can't be certain.' She laid her free hand on his. 'If I'm right, she is not dead. Quite, quite the reverse.'

'What is this?' Honza slumped back, chair rocking and almost overbalancing. The wind and the rain grew hushed.

'I thought you knew.' Imogen freshened the tea in his cup. 'This is the Great Work itself, Honza. This is alchemy.'

After a few hours they went out to get food, a ravenous hunger ambushing Honza in the space between one word and the next. The rain had moved on, leaving the gutters to cluck and gurgle over its antics. A pewter light seeped along each street, loitering in doorways, waving them on to the next bar because there was a familiar face to be found near the window, a conversation to be avoided, walking until a corner pub beckoned them down a flight of steps, old men nodding over their pipes, a dog beside an iron stove barely stirring as they settled in a booth close by. Glass steins of beer, tar-black and slightly sweet. Plates of vegetables, roast and stewed. Mustard pot. The waiter vanished without another word.

His plate was almost empty before Honza sat back, cupping the beer glass in his hands and picking up the conversation where it had paused to let them get food. 'But the dragons.'

'A vision?' Imogen dabbed a napkin to her mouth. 'A waking dream? It's hard to say.'

'It seemed real.'

'It was.' She drank some of her own beer. 'Although not real in the sense we encounter most days.'

'I don't know what to believe.'

'What your instincts tell you to.'

Neither spoke as they finished their meals. Plates cleared, Imogen ordered another round of beers and sat back. 'I felt sure you were involved in something… interesting the first time I saw you at the salon. I didn't realise you know so little of these things.'

'Some of the surrealists dabble—seances and magic rituals—but I never had more than a casual interest. You seem quite expert.'

Imogen shrugged. 'Not all surrealists dabble, I must confess.' She lit a cigarette. 'I'm not as expert as some. Now Godfrey…'

'The man at the salon? Mr Howden?' Honza touched the breast of his jacket.

'Just so.' Imogen nodded. 'When he said he was a collector, Godfrey didn't mean just artworks. It wasn't art that brought him here.'

Honza found Godfrey Howden's calling card in an inside pocket. 'Not me…' He looked at the copperplate script. 'Heavens—' The word threw him against the back of his seat. 'Marietta?'

'Perhaps. I'm inclined to think so.' All Howden had said to her was that an associate had come to this city. 'This associate's presence was enough to make Godfrey come here as quickly as he could. I cheekily asked to tag along and he said yes without thinking. Granted, he would have said yes in almost any event, but his mind was most definitely somewhere else. I didn't give it thought at the time. Now I cannot stop giving it thought. He let things slip, Honza. Dribs and drabs, alas, and this associate—'

She had returned to the hotel she and Howden were staying at, a handful of days before the salon, and found Howden in a foul mood, a reek of Scotch and disappointment clinging to him.

'This associate had visited him earlier that afternoon. "Associate" I gather is very much a euphemism. "Rival" might be closer. Or "adversary".' Imogen swallowed a mouthful of beer. 'It was only after I saw Godfrey's interest in you that I made the leap of connection. The tale of you and your mysterious young woman is quite the gossip in several circles, as I'm sure you know, and I think our being at that salon was due to more than Godfrey's passion for modern art.'

Honza wiped his mouth, emotions tripping over themselves. 'He might…'

'I don't know.' Imogen leaned across the table. 'He might point you in the direction of this associate, who does appear to know something, however.'

'But—' Honza drained his glass. 'This might be coincidence. Or be about someone else. It might…'

Imogen said nothing.

A note waited for Imogen when they reached her hotel. *Sorry to leave without warning or goodbye*, Godfrey Howden had written, his handwriting florid and grandiose, *but there's no point to my being here any longer. You stay on for as long as you like. Do stint on nothing, my dear Im. Your friend, G.*

Honza dropped into a plush seat beside a large potted palm. The hotel lobby chafed. A line of pain cut across his forehead, a diamond-edged knife piercing skin and bone, joints of his knees beginning to ache, his hands tremble. He vowed to give up drinking. He vowed to leave the city, give up art, give up hope. He vowed a hundred things in the space of a dozen rapid heartbeats, wanting to curse Godfrey Howden, anger the sourest taste of all, anger pointless. And still the yearning to grab his misfortune by the scruff of its neck and bellow his misery into its ears, needing to blame someone for how he felt and for what was happening. Needing, even as a part of himself softly cautioned that no such thing would help.

'We missed him by hours,' Honza mumbled.

Imogen nodded, sitting as she held out the note to him. 'There's a postscript.'

> *P.S. If you should cross paths with that young painter we met, Honza Pernath, please remember me to him and offer him my salutations. I should be delighted to speak with him some day. He has such potential.*

The wind spoke in riddles.

Marram grass replied, each word a puzzle to be unpicked, sentences filled with countless meanings always just, just out of reach. Wanting him to wait, to ponder on this sound, that breath or inflection. He dawdled but managed another step. It was hard to get between the dunes this time. The sand moved, hissing, and the sides of the dunes pressed, trying to guide him away from shore and sea. It would be easier to sit and unpick meaning from grass and wind. He tried climbing the face of one of the dunes, sand flowing away beneath hands and feet, carrying backwards, to tumble to the foot of the hill. He was lost, alone in the sand.

The wind grew hushed.

He waited, wanting it to speak again, uncomfortable to be alone with nothing but the sound of his own breathing. He pressed a hand across his mouth. No sound. Until an after-echo stalked over the sands. Not the shout itself but the broken pieces that came after it, the thump of feet.

The dark-haired man stomped over the crest of the dunes, brandishing the black sun over his head, trophy or challenge, black sun flourished as the dark-haired man pointed inland, away from shore and sea. Twisting the sun, the dark-haired man furled it smaller, small enough to fit over the dark-haired man's face, man and sun, sun and man...

Frantic, Honza scrambled up the side of the nearest dune. The breast of sand blocked his view and he had to see the dark-haired man again. The dark-haired man would show him the way inland, away from wind and grass, away from sand and ragged breath. Breath not like the wind, not touched with meaning's edge but simply breath, breath and this clawing at sand and slope, breath loud in Honza's ears, almost loud enough to miss the voice entirely, leave him unsure: did it call from a distance or close to his ear as he foundered towards the dunecrest?

A hand gripped his wrist, heaved.

The dark-haired man thrust his face close and Honza saw himself in the surface sheen of the black sun, face distorted, his features imposing themselves over the face of the dark-haired man visible beneath the black sun, mask beneath mask.

Throat locked. No scream.

The dark-haired man propelled Honza over the crest of the dune: inland, dune mounting on dune, merging into distance and horizon. The voice whispered, words lost in the drag of foot through sand, in the breathing of the dark-haired man. Honza lost, convinced it better to be going somewhere than be lost, better—

The voice whispered, words inaudible.

Honza slipped, fall breaking the dark-haired man's grip,

man trudging on without noticing, huffing and grumbling. Honza, pressed a hand over his mouth, afraid to look back. But, when he turned away from the dark-haired man, he could make out a figure watching from a distant dunecrest, the sea motionless far beyond that, and the black sun low over the waves.

Waiting.

Imogen collected him, a taxi ferrying them to the station, an hour or so before the train. Neither spoke. As he closed the carriage door, she nodded once. 'Good luck,' she told him before walking down the platform, leaving him with nothing to do but sit with his thoughts until the train rocked and trundled out of Prague.

HAMPSTEAD

The man who answered the door was unsure when Godfrey Howden might return.

'It may be days, sir. Or several months. Of course, sir, Mr Howden will send word of his return but, until then…'

'Oh.' Honza looked at the visiting card, the slip of paper in Imogen's crabbed copperplate with directions to this house. Neither could suggest what he should do now.

The man at the door cleared his throat. 'If I might enquire, sir, as to your name?'

'Name?' His mind was blank, empty of everything but dismay. 'Oh… Yes, of course. It's—'

'Dear boy!' A clatter of stout heels, another hail and the woman quite breathless as she halted beside them. 'My dear boy, do—' She fanned her face with her hand. 'Do please excuse me. I thought I'd not find you.'

'Yes…? I don't understand.'

'Of course you don't.' The woman caught her breath. She might have been forty, or older, it was hard to be sure. Her clothes were fashionable—a mustard overcoat and an autumnal three-piece suit beneath—their style neither the most youthful nor quite what a middle-aged woman might adopt, the usual furs replaced by a pashmina of Indian design and no hat, her hair pushed out place by haste and hurry. 'I'm Rose, Rose Greer, and I saw you, as you were on your way here.' Rose Greer indicated the direction Honza had come, following Imogen's instructions. 'I thought I recognised you—there was a good likeness of you in an arts journal last year and—well, anyway, I simply had to intercept you.' She paused. And laughed. 'Intercept you with an offer of hospitality and a helping hand. You've discovered Godfrey is out of town, I should say.'

The man at the door gave a polite cough. 'Miss Greer, I believe Mr Howden may have left instructions regarding this gentleman—'

'No doubt, Mr Danvers.' Rose Greer smiled at Honza. 'No saying when he'll return. In the meantime, do let me see if I can help you.'

'Mr Howden's instructions, Miss, are—'

'Please, Danvers, don't concern yourself.' Rose waved away Mr Danvers's qualms. 'I've communicated with Godfrey. Recently.' She fixed her attention on Honza. 'Do, please, allow me to help.'

Rose's house lay at the end of a narrow side road, an impudent breeze kicking leaves along the gutter as they drove past stolid houses and villas fending off the road with short lengths of garden, shrubberies cowed and prim. Trees peered over a high wall as they slowed at the end of the lane, top storeys of a house squinting at them through branches growing skeletal and black. Rose clambered out of the roadster and opened the wooden gates.

She had insisted on collecting his suitcase from the hotel—'I have plenty of room and you'll not disturb any more than you'll impose, I assure you'—before driving them out of the centre of London. 'Where are we?' Honza had asked as they neared the side road, the house among the trees waiting for them at its end. Rose had laughed. 'Hampstead. Frightfully staid, I know. I'll show you Marx's tomb later, if you like.' And she had laughed again.

She laughed a lot. At the world; as often as not at herself. Honza found himself liking her, although the speed of events left no time for reflection.

The house stood amidst a sprawling garden, wall and trees making for seclusion and, even with the neighbours visible in the near distance, it was easy to think this was a country estate, far beyond the city, the house calm and wearing the air of something rooted and used to being a part of this place.

Aside from Rose, only Jeni, her housekeeper, lived in the house. Jeni was a plumper, older version of Rose and, since they hardly bothered with formalities and had obviously known each other for years, they could have been sisters instead of employer and employee. Rose led him to the kitchen, Jeni setting out cheese and fresh bread for them all, coffee brewing on the stove as omelettes sizzled. 'Eat,' Rose said, 'then tell me everything.'

Honza sat back. 'And that's when you found me.' He was surprised to find the last of the coffee cold and forgotten in his cup, Jeni sitting at the other end of the table, quietly shelling peas as she listened, flint-edged light coming through the kitchen windows with promises of dusk and a chill night to come.

Rose reached across the table and gave his hand a comforting squeeze. 'That's quite a tale. You must be utterly exhausted.'

'I'm sure it all sounds very melodramatic.' The house felt poised around them as it picked over his story. Honza frowned. 'Or insane.'

'Not a bit.' Rose grew thoughtful and the silence was filled with Jeni's preparations for the evening meal. 'I don't know this associate of Godfrey's, beyond knowing there's a certain rivalry between them. But I agree that Godfrey's hotfooting to Prague on word of this associate's appearance and your young lady's unexpected departure around the same time are suggestive of there being a link between the two. At least that there's an interest in it all on Godfrey's part.'

'How long might he be away?'

'Oh months. Very easily.' Rose patted his hand again as he slumped in his chair. 'You're most welcome to stay here as long as you like. Unless you have business in Prague? No? Then be my guest, Honza, for as long as you wish. And…' Rose turned to Jeni. 'What do you think?'

'Can't say.' Jeni paused, pea pod squeezed open between her fingers. 'Be worth a try though.'

Honza tried to push away hope, although it pulled at his face and forced him to sit up, focus shifting between the two women as he asked, 'What?'

The low building stood some way down the garden. It might have been a potting shed in an earlier incarnation, the iron chimney rearing out of its side obviously a later addition.

Rose rattled keys into sturdy mortice locks. 'The local children sometimes try to get in on a dare.'

She pushed open the door and a waft of warm, slightly humid air drew him inside. Honza was not sure what he was expecting. Still this chemist's laboratory struck him as absurd. Bottles and jars lined the walls. A Bunsen burner rumbled, vapour coating the flask it fiercely heated. Elsewhere, liquids dripped, oozed through tangles of pipes with unfathomable purpose.

All that was missing were sparks and a few pieces of dazzling electrical equipment.

Rose perched on a stool and watched as he moved around the laboratory, reluctant to get too close to the equipment although curiosity had replaced his initial surprise, no matter that a tinge of disappointment lay acid in his stomach.

'Here.' Rose disconnected a flask from the pipe feeding it and drew out a little pale yellow liquor with a pipette. A few drops went into a small tumbler. Water from a stillage. A pinch of powder scraped from a crucible: just a pinch, black against limpid gold, fading as it dissolved.

She held out the concoction. 'Here.'

He hesitated.

'Please.'

Honza took the tumbler. Sniffed. And caught whiff of something that reminded him of nothing so much as a summer's day in the country.

The smell was not there on second breath, only the flat scent of water made pungent by a passing hint of alcohol. And the flavour also vanished before he knew it might be there. He waited. Drained the rest of the glass and waited again. Nothing. And he was about to say so when the acid in his stomach faded and a little of the tension in his shoulders loosened, tension he had not been aware of carrying.

These were more than simple medicines.

Jeni brought in tea, tray set on the low table between the old but welcoming armchairs they had installed themselves in after Rose had shown him a little more of the laboratory and they had come back to this small, book-lined study.

Spagyrics—the alchemy of plants.

Impossible to scoff as Rose spoke of the soul of plants revealed by diligent repetitions: washings, heatings, distillations and recombinations, over and over until the deepest essence of all was freed. Impossible because Honza had not felt so calm for weeks, stomach muscles relaxed, the Gordian knot they had wound into gently teased apart, the bite of acid bile at the pit of his throat suddenly gone.

Rose handed him a steaming cup. Honza thanked her, attention caught by the corner of the laboratory just visible through the French windows.

'It's all—' He cleared his throat. For over an hour they had sat and Rose had talked about her work, Honza asking few questions, mostly listening, aware of the gradual relaxation of muscle and mood. Still, there was an urge to be rational, practical… 'It does sound far-fetched. In this day and age, I mean.'

'I used to think so.' Rose watched him over the lip of her cup, steam blurring her face. 'And yet.'

'And yet,' he agreed. The urge to be rational meant very little against how he felt. And yet the true reason he had to accept all this was because it was so much like the things Marietta had spoken of.

'One Art,' Rose nodded, 'and, at heart, One Path. Your friend was coming to understand this, I suspect.'

More than simple medicines, because they held within them a spark of something otherwise hidden. Rose spoke of quintessence, or a virtue, a vital, living essence. *A light at the centre of each substance*, Rose had said, *a wondrous flame that can heal. And more.*

Wondrous. Just as Marietta had said.

But what about Howden and this rival of his?

'I've heard rumours.' Rose indicated he should help himself to as much food as he wished. Jeni poured glimmering wine, pale as first light, into their glasses and softly closed the dining room door behind her.

'The best I can offer is a guess.' Rose touched a napkin to her lips. The scents of roast vegetables and mustard, of steamed cabbage (the smell of something buried in the earth and beginning, gently, to ferment) filled each breath. Honza added a little salt, the absence of meat not registering as he ate another mouthful, simply accepting it as given, ever since Marietta, ever since she had left. He paused. Took another mouthful and let the sensations of taste and texture, the motion of jaw and tongue, flow, one over the next as a musical theme and variation might flow. He sipped wine and nodded at the wine's brilliance, and that Rose was more than welcome to guess.

'Undoubtedly a passage in the Great Work is taking place.' She took another mouthful of food, considering as she chewed. 'Yes. It must be.'

Darkness came to the dining room window. Dusk had been pottering about the laboratory and weaving between the trees when they had finished tea and Rose suggested he might want to rest before dinner. Only candles lit the dining room, flittering light mesmerised by its own reflection in the darkened glass.

Honza frowned. 'Lead into gold?'

'Figuratively, yes, something of the sort. But alchemist's lead is not ordinary lead and our gold is not ordinary gold, either.'

'I don't understand.'

Rose leaned forward, holding up her glass so that it gathered candlelight.

'Physical transformation is the foundation of the Art—you've seen a little in the laboratory and that route, working with plants, is commonly known as the Lesser Path: an end in itself but also, potentially, a training to set the alchemist towards the Greater Path—lead into gold, as you say, the transformation of metals.'

She turned the glass between her fingers and the wine cast candlelight in a dozen directions, light subtly changed by its encounter with the wine. For an instant Honza thought he saw sunlight on grape vines filling a sleeping hillside, someone in the distance waving to him.

'But—' Rose took a sip of the wine. 'But at each stage, there are more than simple chemical reactions taking place. That would confine us to the chemist's laboratory, a place where the transformations of the Art are impossible.'

She moved the wine glass again and Honza watched the light bob, dart, turn about itself, wind murmuring as it brushed over the vines, words lost in the shimmering of leaf and stem thrilled at the wind's touch. There were foothills behind him and a presence he could not see. In the distance, someone waved but he took no notice.

'Spirit,' Rose told him. 'The alchemist puts some of their spirit into the work. Some call it the Secret Fire, Honza, that part of each of us that links us to higher states of consciousness, to the cosmos itself.'

Candlelight reached out to run a finger down the side of the glass. A clock had been ticking out in the hallway. It fell silent and there was no saying how long it was before Honza managed to speak.

'I've never heard of a secret fire.'

'And yet you know it very well, Honza.' Rose put down

her glass. The clock chimed the half-hour and the candle flames settled back into themselves.

'The imagination.' She smiled as she picked up knife and fork and began eating again. 'That wonderful capacity we all have to create beauty and find its source in commonplace things. Or create things that could not have existed otherwise.

'The Imagination.' Rose waved a hand towards him. 'The *ignis innaturalis*, the secret fire itself and something you're very used to dealing with, Honza.'

A tawny owl called, speaking of loss, lamentations to the sky and to the night.

'I knew her only a short time, a few months.'

Light from the house brushed against Rose's face, hardly separating her from the shadows.

The owl called again.

'It's ridiculous to feel this for someone I barely knew.'

'I think,' Rose began and for a few moments her voice might have been the breeze through oak and hazel, might have been the leaves drifting to rest on the damp grass. 'I think you knew her better than you believe.'

'I'm sorry.' Honza drew a deep breath and shook himself. 'I might have had more to drink than I realised. I enjoyed dinner, though, thank you.'

'You're welcome.'

The owl made no comment.

Honza stood awkwardly, unsure if Rose was about to say something more or if he should excuse himself and go to bed. He remembered enjoying their meal but recalled very little of what they had said, unsure why he had begun talking about Marietta when Rose had suggested a breath of air, a few minutes under the stars. The sky was bottomless—hard to believe London surrounded the house; aside from a small lamp beside the French windows, there was only the faintest sliver of moon remaining to give light, not even the street lamps at the mouth of the cul-de-sac showed through the trees.

They might be anywhere, far from anywhere.

The owl spoke to the stars and to the night and its loneliness was as bottomless as the sky, each star isolated from those apparently close beside it by countless years, inconceivable distances.

'I think,' Rose began and her voice was the branches of the oak trees creaking, was the leaves brushing against the damp, heady grass. 'I think your friend is well along the Path, following the way towards the Great Work, Honza. She transforms herself, her spirit, her essence.'

The night reached out and rested a consoling hand on his shoulder.

'She is moving beyond the surface world we live in, this material world with its industries and its politics and its self-absorbed way of experiencing life, which is to see without depth.'

Honza felt himself sag, stomach growing tight as grief rose to catch in his throat.

'I can't find her again,' he managed.

The owl sighed.

'One Art, one Path.'

Oak and hazel nodded to him.

'You must follow that Path.'

Dull light peered through a gap in the curtains, urging him to get up, get up. Honza rolled out of bed and pushed open the curtain. Clouds smeared the sky, London knitting smoke into a cowl, a grey haze that made time uncertain and every edge provisional, unfinished.

He took a breath. Waiting for a hangover's weight to settle and finding trepidation and doubt, mostly an expectation that set a tremor through his fingers and made each button an effort to fasten, and which recast the eyes staring back at him from the bathroom mirror—not quite a stranger's, although they seemed unlike the expression that had been reflected back to him these past weeks.

Rose smiled as she looked up from the charts and papers spread across her desk. 'Come in, do.' She waved him into her study and tapped a finger on the charts: horoscopes and what appeared to be astronomical tables. 'Propitious alignments are crucial—do you understand astrology, at all?'

Honza shook his head.

'The influences are subtle. The charts indicate energy flows within the solar system and greater cosmos, and those flows find correspondence within us and vice versa, hence the old adage, *As Above, So Below*.' When Honza continued to look uncertain, Rose suggested: 'Think of a sailor planning when to leave harbour by consulting a tide table.' She touched star chart, horoscope, almanac. 'These are our tide tables.'

'And?' Honza pulled up a chair, peering at astronomical symbols and columns of figures.

'We're in luck. Whatever brought you to me was a fine judge of timing. Have you breakfasted?'

'No.'

'Good, then we begin at once.' Rose clapped her hands.

It began to rain.

Rain beat against the laboratory roof.

A period of fasting was important.

Rose tightened the tourniquet around his arm as she explained.

It meant for a purer specimen. And no meat in his diet for some time was very helpful, very.

He watched the needle, blood flow from vein to small flask, and felt only excitement.

Rain beat against the laboratory roof.

A damp wind insinuated itself into the house, tapping on his bedroom door for attention, or slipping in without being noticed to paw at his ankles and neck. Honza ignored it, turning another page.

Rose had lent him books on alchemy. They drew him in through their illustrations, phantasmagorias as strange as anything Marie and her colleagues created, more so in fact because he thought they hinted that wonders were to be found in the waking world, in things commonplace without resort to dream or trance or even happenstance, without any of the methods used by surrealists to uncover the marvellous. Yet the texts accompanying the pictures failed to enlighten as to how this might be so and Honza grew frustrated with what seemed to be deliberate evasions and obfuscations, the authors (all practicing alchemists, he assumed) making vague what had appeared to be so much simpler in the illustrations. But the leap, from intuitive sense of something there to be understood and understanding itself, that was nowhere to be found.

The change will be slow.

Honza watched the flask as Rose moved about the laboratory behind him. His blood rippled, flame beneath the flask driving off liquid to ghost along the neck of the bottle and into an angled pipe.

Will I feel anything? he asked at some point.

No, not a thing, she told him as she measured out several drops of this, something of that, into a small beaker, rehydrating dried leaves and grinding them, filtering the result, a pipette drawing a little filtrate and adding—*drop*—a touch—*drop*—to the beaker.

The blood above the flame moved, a little condensation rolling back—*drop… drop*—from the shoulders of the flask and the pipework attached to it.

That will come later, she told him, and in good time, don't worry.

I'll try not to…

But?

Honza focused on the flask but he could picture Rose, at a bench behind him, glancing up, a small glass funnel in one hand, beaker and a sapphire blue ampule waiting.

I'm willing to believe, he told her.

But it's difficult not to doubt. Rose folded filter paper into funnel, poured a little, a little more, from the small beaker across the paper, to filter—*drop… drop*—into the ampule.

This will help.

The blue glass was cool in his palm.

It strengthens what's already there. Psychologically speaking. Protects the resolve from doubt.

Rose had him roll up his sleeve as she spoke, inspecting yesterday's catheter mark before taking a freshly sterilised needle and sliding it into a different location.

Just a few drops, each day.

Honza thought she meant blood, not the blue ampule, the preparation to help the resolve.

Rain hammered against the laboratory door but he did not hear it.

They drove into town and Rose took him for afternoon tea at Claridge's.

'I don't do this very often.' She sat back as the waiter refreshed their tea pot and returned with another round of dainty sandwiches. 'It's an occasional indulgence.'

Honza nibbled a watercress sandwich and sipped tea. 'Very nice.'

Rose laughed. 'A perfectly English description.'

'Sorry, I didn't mean—'

'Hush.' She patted his hand. 'I'm teasing. Still, this is a very English custom.'

Honza looked about the dining room. Men with precisely parted hair, pinstripe suits and unbending postures. Women wreathed in perfume and fox fur, expressions animate or fixed. All, he thought, missing something, hypnotised by—

He refocused on Rose, the thought gone in any case. 'You don't think of yourself as English.' He had meant it as a question, not a statement. Rose shook her head, her own expression obscure.

'Scottish, Honza, I'm a Scot. "Greer" you see. Nothing of the Norman to be found in me, a Celt at heart.'

'I met someone in Praha, Prague, I mean, who called herself a Celt. Another friend of Mr Howden's, Imogen—Imogen Carwithen—do you know her?'

'Oh, Miss Carwithen. Yes. Such a frightfully precocious young woman. How thrilling of you to have made her acquaintance.'

In the tea room at Claridge's it seemed the sun might always shine, even at night.

Jeni brought him lunch.

'I can come downstairs, I feel fine.'

'It's no trouble, Mr Honza, truly.' Jeni set the tray on the coffee table at the foot of the bed.

'Please call me Honza.' He threw back the sheets and tried to leap from bed to prove how well he was. Dizziness pushed him back against the mattress and told him to wait a moment.

'You'll be fine soon, Rose says, and she's sure to be right. But for now...' Jeni helped him into a dressing gown and led him to the armchair. The house had become haunted by the dank chill, which waited at the bedside as he dozed and found its way into his dreams. Not that he remembered his dreams these days, just fleeting impressions that vanished once he came round.

Five days like this. Not the cold he had thought it was at first, nor the 'flu. Just a phase, Rose had declared, all to be expected. Meanwhile, she continued her work. Can you explain it? he asked and Rose said: Read the books, come to an understanding, then we talk when you're better. But

Honza slept, or dozed, the dank chill wandering the room, or thumbing through memories—of childhood, of books read or put aside, of past loves, past friends, of painting most of all. Of the feel of charcoal between fingers and paper, or the smell of pigment as the pallet knife drew one colour into another, two becoming a third and that third tinting, shading, recalling the first colour as it grew into a fourth, muscles moving, breath drawn in, exhaling shape, form, imagination inseparable from joint, sinew, bone, muscle, flesh and skin and canvas…

Five days like this. Damp chill and a wind maundering along the ridge tiles, plucking at the window sash or slamming a door somewhere in the house.

Jeni took the cover off the lunch plate. Kale, steamed, and leeks in butter, with beetroot, all under a generous sprinkle of parsley, with nettle tea steaming in a pot.

'This will soon set you right.' She smiled as she closed the door behind her.

Condensation dripped down glass.

Honza waited, expecting rain. The window remained dry, no matter how dark the clouds grew.

The damp chill touched his shoulder and he pushed away the image, the sensation of humidity and dew against his skin, and began to eat.

Self-consciously, he stopped talking.

'Please tell me the rest.' Rose uncrossed her ankles and leaned forward in her armchair to pour more tea from the pot.

'I feel…' He peered into the tea cup, steam touching his face with fingers that smelled metallic, cup heavy, fingers and hands complaining as he put the cup down again, untouched. A taste had lingered in his mouth for days, so bad he could no more than pick at dinner. Honza pushed the cup a little further away across the occasional table beside his chair.

'I feel…' In the hallway outside the sitting room the clock droned, monotonous, as he was sure he must sound, reciting another memory, another anecdote. All about someone else. 'I must be outstaying my welcome.'

'Not a bit, don't think that for even a moment, Honza. You mustn't. You won't,' Rose instructed. Kindly, just as she listened to tales of himself, himself and Marietta, kindly. 'We are on the Path together, Honza. We'll see it to the end together.' And the candlelight (always candlelight) and the glow from the sitting room fire (never quite warm enough to keep away the damp chill) brought her face from the shadows and it was harder than ever to guess her age, in spite of lines around her eyes and mouth, in spite of the sag of skin here and there, which should have been a tally of years accrued but in this light they diverted her away from time's flow and left her in some place neither quite now, neither quite then…

The thought faded into the snap of the fire, the taste of iron, scent of tea. 'If you're sure.' If she wanted to hear these stories, even if they felt on his tongue as if they belonged to someone else—

'Of course I want to hear your memories, Honza,' she reassured him. 'You know—' Rose clapped her hands as she spoke— 'you need to do something different, see some faces other than mine and Jeni's. How about a party? We could go up to town. I have a friend who would loan us a flat for a few days. You could go to galleries or museums, or whatever you wished, and we could have a get-together so you can meet new people. A small get-together,' Rose added, seeing his uncertainty. 'A change of setting and of pace will do wonders.'

He hesitated. 'The Work?'

'Will be fine.' Rose smiled. 'In a few days. When you feel better. You'll feel better soon.'

Honza nodded. The clock in the hall paused.

The damp wind knew the books were nonsense. Honza turned a page and a man, half red, half black, stepped from a deep pool towards a queen, her skin alabaster, a star fixed above her head. She waited for the man part red, part black, his features obscured, red like a dawning day.

The words made no sense.

Yes, the damp presence murmured.

Honza shivered, tips of each finger numb with cold, although the fire cracked and blazed.

On another page, a black sun gave light to rolling countryside, hillsides transparent so the sun was visible through a haze of earth and tree as if the black sun were a part of the earth and of the landscape, not a distant star at all but a quality close to hand, hidden but present.

It no longer looked marvellous to Honza.

(The presence nodded: this was so.)

He could not see wonders, could not understand why he had thought there was anything wondrous in these images. He pushed away the book. (The presence caught it as it fell from the arm of the chair, set it out of reach.) The authors were deliberately obscuring nothing. There was nothing, Honza grumbled, nothing to obscure.

(The presence said nothing.)

It sat beside him, the presence, dank and grey. Sat beside him each night as he tried to sleep, a nurse tending to the sick. It spoke to him. The words slipped from his mind, left nothing but a faint mustiness which settled into the fissures of his skull, the base of his neck, and added to his exhaustion.

And I don't sleep, he said, haven't slept in a week.

Honza turned away from the presence to the man, part red, part black. I'm asleep?

Yes. You do sleep, for an hour or two each night. We don't often have chance to talk, though.

They stood at the foot of the bed, beside the pool, its waters picking up a silvery sheen, although there was no moon, sky grey, perhaps empty, perhaps obscured. Grey.

She will not come.

Honza startled. He had not realised how hard, how long, he had been staring at the water.

Rose?

No. The man, part red, part black, rested a hand on Honza's arm, squeezing gently. She—the queen, the angel. She will not come.

At all? And Honza felt his feet sinking into the earth at the edge of the pool. Not anchoring. Miring.

She has not gone for good.

I've been trying to find her, to follow her. Do you know what's happening? I don't have to explain it all, do I? all that's happened?

You do not have to explain anything. The man, part red, part black, walked around the edge of the pool, peering down into the grey. Distant or close, Honza could not see anything. The man pointed.

Are you sure this is the way?

It's the one I'm following.

The man, part red, part black, tilted his head to one side as he studied at Honza. Honza stammered, There's only one Path and that's to follow her, to become the way she is, one Path, one Art.

She will not come, was all the man said.

I— I don't think that's true.

She will not come. And the man, part red, part black, rested a hand on his arm again.

But, if I follow, I won't have to wait for her to come. Honza felt the dirt beneath him sag, cling tighter. He spoke more quickly, needing to convince. If I follow I can catch up, I can find her along the Path, I can—

The words were smoke. The man, part red, part black, took no notice. He shook his head. The star, he explained, and the sea.

The— The star and the sea?

Honza had forgotten.

The man, part red, part black, nodded to the horizon.

A sun, black, visible through hillsides visible only because the black sun was visible through them.

The black sun opened its eyes.

Honza screamed. Pushed the man away. Pushed himself away, dank earth opening. A familiar blanket falling away to leave him blinking at grey light behind the curtains, bedroom cold because the fire had burned out in the night. Sleep, as it had been for days, impossible.

Only blackness in the flask.

'Look closer.' Rose pointed, careful not to touch the hot glass. 'There. See?'

Honza could not. Heat from the athanor prickled his face as he leaned closer. 'I… Oh—' It had looked like condensation. 'That white spot?'

Rose nodded. Honza found he was smiling, the first smile he had worn in weeks. Months.

'That,' Rose confirmed, 'is the next stage in the Work. It's happening.' She was filled with energy, with enthusiasm. Honza could not shake his own smile.

'I'm very grateful. This is so generous and kind. You don't know me and yet—'

Dizziness embraced him, laboratory bowing in deference to this superior force, flowing about him, a whirlpool of glassware and benches. Honza managed to clutch hold of a passing stool.

'It won't last long. It's to be expected.' Rose helped him to a chair, easing his head down towards his knees until the pulse in his ears thrummed less, dizziness ebbing, to well, to ebb further. 'The Elixir draws strength from you.' She helped Honza sit back before going to the shelves, making a preparation as she continued, 'You're linked together, as I've explained, but the vitality it takes from you the Elixir eventually returns in its own way, tenfold.' She stirred the preparation. 'Or ten-thousandfold.'

'Better?' she asked once he had managed to keep down the preparation and a few minutes had passed. Honza told her he was and swivelled towards the flask.

'This will take me to Marietta.'

'The Elixir is already a long step along the Path. It's already powerful. But, Honza, it will be more so once we've finished this Work. Lead into Gold—or Base risen towards the Divine.'

'The everyday into the marvellous.'

'Yes.' Rose pulled up a stool and gave him a pat on the knee. 'You learned something from those books I lent you, then?'

There might be a dozen, more, memories to choose from but he saw her at a small gallery, a friend's private showing, sunlight streaming through a skylight transforming her as she spoke, *The mundane into the marvellous.*

'Not really.' Honza shrugged.

'No matter. You understand as well as any adept: the Elixir will unlock the star within, lift the soul back to the Heavens.' Rose laughed with delight. 'All rather exciting, isn't it?'

Honza said it was, distracted again by a thought that vanished each time he reached for it.

Rose rubbed her hands together. They would go up to town at the week-end. It was time, she told him.

Streets thick with umbrellas, rain hissed beneath the tyres and slithered across the windscreen, wiper blades reaping spray with each scythe across the glass. A droplet wove an erratic path down the passenger window, pausing often, perhaps running on in the direction it had been or diverting but still downwards, oozing down. Abruptly, the droplet rose hurriedly up the glass, to leap into the air, vanish.

A glimmer of white fluttered in the rain.

Honza startled.

'What month is it?'

'You have plenty of time before you need to worry about Christmas shopping.' Rose smiled at her own joke, the car slowing to stop at a red light.

Honza searched but could find no other sign of snow.

The flat was tastefully decorated in a Neoclassical style. It felt as though no one ever lived there. Or, if they did, they never exhibited any personality within its walls. It was more like stage set.

'It's very elegant,' Honza told Rose when she asked.

It was only a little after midday and Rose led him on a short walk to a restaurant where a group of her friends met them for lunch. Honza found himself sitting immediately to Rose's right, Rose at the head of the table. A flush of discomfort kept him all but silent as menus were consulted, small talk made, aperitifs sipped. Of course, he reasoned, he wasn't on show, it was natural curiosity amongst Rose's friends. She had made introductions but the names were gone already. He glanced up from the menu. An elderly woman, directly opposite, wrinkled, spare, a huge amethyst in a silver setting pinned to her tweed jacket, smiled and wondered if he was having as much difficulty choosing as she. Honza mumbled something in agreement and the man next to him advised they should have the mullet.

'Best course, when there's doubt.' His stare was intense, skin pale, untouched by sunlight in years, a mop of greying hair presiding over a face gaunt enough to suggest he rarely made the acquaintance of food in general, let alone this restaurant's board of fair.

'You're my guest today, Robin.' Rose peered over her own menu. 'Choose just exactly what you wish.'

'Mullet.' Robin put down his menu. And tugged at his pinched cheeks. 'Or the lamb.'

Rose turned to Honza. 'You two might find common ground. You're both artists.'

Honza thought it would be polite to say Oh, that's

interesting, but catching Robin's gaze, found he had to look away. Several of the other guests offered courteous nods or greetings as he glanced down the table, none apparently as strange as the man beside him. At the far end of the table sat a woman closer to his own age. Her complexion was a deft shade of walnut and her features Persian, or possibly Arab, untouched by make-up, her hair hidden beneath a scarf of dove grey silk, although her clothes were European. She settled her own gaze on him and, in that first instant, it was as if her eyes were black, a pure obsidian polished and lustrous and warmed by the sun, not cold stone at all. Surprise made Honza look again, discover black was deep teak, no less lustrous.

The woman inclined her head, a nod of greeting but no smile. Instead—

Robin laid a hand on Honza's wrist.

'I've seen your work. In the journals.'

'Oh. Yes?'

And the woman with the amethyst broach told him she had seen one of his canvases. In Paris, would it have been?

The main course appeared without leaving memory of the first.

'I see you also don't eat meat, Mein Herr,' the lady with the amethyst observed, 'like Rose.'

'Not for a while, no.' The food looked delicious. He had no memory of choosing it. 'Please call me Honza.'

'They make it for me when I come here.' Rose indicated their plates. 'I took the liberty of ordering for us both. You seemed to be having a hard time deciding.'

'Nothing wrong with flesh.' Robin attacked the pigeon he had chosen. 'In moderation.'

'You sound to be trying to convince yourself,' the woman with the amethyst broach laughed.

Honza felt bile rise and sipped water. Only he and Rose and the Persian woman were not drinking alcohol. He pretended to be looking around the dining room, finding her deep in conversation with the people beside her, and uncertain why he should disguise his curiosity.

Food sat heavily in his stomach.

'I don't think I'm quite ready for this, after all,' he whispered to Rose.

'Oh, do eat what you can.' She brushed his hair away from his eyes. 'Don't worry if it's too much, though. But do wait for dessert. It's another speciality.' She patted his hand and he felt comforted. And the dessert was mint sorbet flavoured with nutmeg, other species he could not identify. Nausea abated enough to tempt him to ask for another bowl.

'I'm afraid I must be going but thank you for your hospitality and for inviting me to join your party this afternoon.'

The Persian woman nodded goodbye to the company and thanked Rose again before she walked from the dining room. For a moment, he wondered if she had looked at him at all. Wondered why it should matter.

'There is more of the sorbet. Another serving?' Rose held out a hand in invitation.

'No.' Honza dropped his napkin across the empty bowl. 'No, thank you. I've had enough.'

The party was the following evening. Robin came early, a lugubrious ghost that haunted the corner of the room Honza found himself in, talking of brush technique and creating pigments from raw materials ('revealing the spirit of colour from within base matter' Robin called it), or unreeling a tangled exposition on the soul and its expression through painting. At one point, Honza asked if Robin knew anything of alchemy, was perhaps a practitioner of some sort. Robin stared from beneath his mop of hair and mumbled that true adepts never spoke of their Art.

Now and then Rose introduced guests to Honza, breaking Robin's flow. Their names and faces hardly registered, Honza wishing he was not so tired; his joints had ached all day and he wondered if he was getting a cold. If he had more energy he would make an excuse, escape Robin. Instead, he sat, picking at the food that had appeared on the small table beside him.

At last Robin declared he was ravenous and would go in search of the buffet table. Honza claimed he was happy sitting where he was, willing Robin out of the room. But, as he was about to heave himself from the chair, the woman with the amethyst broach appeared. She reintroduced herself as she sat, asking if he remembered her from yesterday. Of course he did, she assured him. Honza dragged his face into an approximation of a smile, aware that, although she had said it only seconds before, he still could not remember her name.

After a few minutes, more people joined them, two women, a man, all people Rose had introduced earlier and all of them with names that had darted away and left no trace.

Exhaustion took his shoulders and pushed him further into his seat as the others sat in a half circle of faces moving, talking, features never quite registering. Honza took a mouthful of food, hoping eating would make him feel better. No taste, little texture. Putting aside his plate, he stared across the room, through the open doorway to the room beyond, searching from face to face. Finding Rose and sure he had not been looking for her at all.

'... or daimon,' one of the women was saying.

'Something like a star, I've always thought,' the man replied, 'an internal star.'

'To navigate by?' Honza asked, uncertain what prompted him to speak.

'A guiding light, as it were.' The man fixed his gaze on Honza, long enough for it to become uncomfortable, silence lengthening until the woman with the amethyst broach began to speak lightly of an exhibition, a simply fascinating exhibition, that was on at the moment.

'We must go,' she told Honza. 'Tomorrow.'

'Of course you must.'

'But—' He had hardly slept, despite exhaustion worming into every joint and the space between every thought.

'The distraction—the stimulation—will do you good,' Rose assured him, placing a small glass next to his largely untouched breakfast. A dull sheen lay over the surface of the water.

'Drink,' she told him.

She showed him to the gallery but had plans of her own and left him to go in alone. A mist turned lazy dervish circles in the wake of a passing taxi. The air smelled of soot and left greasy marks as it pawed his face. Honza watched Rose turn the far corner of the road and thought how much he would enjoy a few hours alone.

The lobby door made a flourish and revealed the woman with the amethyst broach sitting and reading. She waved a greeting.

'Robin said he might call by later.'

The damp presence slipped in behind Honza, just before the lobby door closed.

No Robin. One of the women from the party did accompany them. Dimly, Honza thought she might have been at the lunch too. She remembered herself to him, including her name. A smile of greeting and her name wriggled from his hand, scurrying into the shadows under a radiator. The morning went in much the same way. Canvases made salaams of greeting, dissecting themselves into myriad cubist blocks before making excuses and slipping from memory, empty space to be filled by the next painting. His companions alternated between respectful silence and animated, whispered discussions, none of which found any purchase on his mind and when they asked his opinion,

Honza had no idea what he was saying.

They seemed not to notice.

The gallery adopted a worshipful expression, hands behind its back as it conducted them from room to room, respectfully indicating this drawing, that canvas.

The presence passed over each one and rendered it grey.

'Simply divine—'

The woman with the amethyst broach had spoken, a huge canvas in the next room a lodestone drawing the two women into its sphere. Honza turned away, noticing a side corridor, a small room beyond, a pair of spotlights creating a shadowless space around a single painting.

An angel stood on the edge of a golden ocean, scintillating halo burnishing the waters, waves paused to regard this radiant being come to earth—

No, Honza, I have come out of the water, climbed onto the shore to feel the sand between my toes, be in contact with the earth, with the air, be part of this world. And there is this…

But no angel had spoken. He was sure he had thought those words.

Honza looked beyond the edge of the spotlights, back along the deserted corridor.

He must have thought the words. No one else could have spoken—

And there is this…

The angel held out both hands so he could see…

Astrum…

It happened again on each of the next few days. Rose encouraged him to go out, stroll, take in the sights, while she attended to some matter, some little business or such, and Honza would trudge out, into rain, or sodden leaves flailed by a sharp-tempered wind, the grey day smirched with soot as every chimney made burnt offerings to the coming winter, Honza taking little notice, exhaustion clinging him to him, ardent and unwilling to let him go, wanting all his attention and affection, wanting all of him, relenting only when the dank, whispering presence returned, often unnoticed at first, so used was he to its voice, so used that voice might be his own, much as the presence seemed a part of each joint that popped and creaked, each stiff and weak muscle, indistinguishable, inseparable, simply: him, and Honza decided it must be grief, nothing else, and so he trudged out when Rose suggested he should, no desire to walk, or take in the sights, with no desire aside from a wan, flickering gratitude towards Rose for all her effort and help, and so he trudged out to please her. No desire other than that. Except for time to be alone.

He never was. Robin would happen by. By accident. The woman with the amethyst broach would be passing in a cab and stop and insist on keeping him company. Or they might appear together, accompanied by someone who had met him at the lunch or the party, the gallery... it was beside the point where, he never remembered their faces, their names, only an impression of their presence that lingered, a taste on the back of the tongue or a pressure over his eyes.

Friday.
'I thought another party tonight.' Rose skimmed over the front page of the morning paper on the table beside her and returned to her breakfast. 'To see us off tomorrow, back to the house. Smaller than last time,' she added when he made no comment.

Honza sipped the tincture she had made him, his own breakfast untouched. The presence spoke for him. 'That would be lovely.'

'Settled then.' Rose pressed a napkin to her lips and pushed back her chair. 'I'll make the arrangements now. I have a few other things to do but we could meet for tea this afternoon?'

Honza nodded.
'You'll walk?'

Honza nodded.

'Good.'

Honza nodded, pulling the front door closed behind him and waiting at the corner, no destination in mind but resigned that someone would find him soon, whichever way he took.

Good. The presence was satisfied.

Turning the corner. Cars, a dray, two delivery vans, cyclists. One of them was bound to be…

The presence agreed: why fight?

Scuffing over uneven flagstones, traffic coughing and wheezing against the chimney smoke weaving phantoms on the chill air. The presence made no comment. Honza took another step.

And walked out into the road.

A bus sounded its horn, driver shaking his fist as he put the contraption back into gear. Honza stumbled into the curb, almost toppling onto the pavement, bus accelerating, passengers a blur, conductor leaning out the back and warning him to bloody well wake up. Asking, 'You alright, guv'nor?'

Too shocked. To find breath. Hands shaking. Knees un— unsteady. Pulse thunderous.

Honza managed to wave. Wave almost pitching him to the ground, balance pirouetting with the road and the buildings. Eyes squeezed. Shut. Breath. Breathe. Ragged breaths. Clammy skin, stomach knotting.

A voice, close to one ear, suggested, 'It's safe to cross but hurry.'

Honza hurried.

'Alley.'

Honza followed. Across the road at the end of the alley, along a short mews, on to a bus, fumbling over change so the conductor had to help, trip only two stops, to climb off, dodge up another alley, walk a back street slowly, so there was chance to catch breath.

'It must be a relief to be on your own.'

Honza agreed, the voice familiar. The street was empty; it was good to be on his own.

'They won't find you for a while yet,' the voice assured him. Honza thought of Marie's expedition. The voice made no reply, only suggested he get on the next bus and left him to his thoughts as Honza gazed out the window, sky no less grey but the breeze drier and sharper, suggesting the weather might be about to turn.

'Might have snow,' the woman sitting next to him agreed.

Honza got off along Oxford Street. 'British Museum that way.' The conductor pointed along the road. 'You'll see the signs.'

'Thank you.' Honza followed the conductor's directions until a sign indicated he should take a turning.

A bookshop watched from across the road. Symbols decorated the covers displayed in the window. A crystal ball on one side, an incense burner in the opposite corner.

'Go inside.'

A brass bell clattered and mingled incense, jasmine and patchouli, greeted him and ushered him in. Music played, crackling, a gramophone in the back of the shop, piano intense and haunted, angular dreams lying between each cluster of notes. A kettle whistled and someone hummed in approximation of the notes on the record. Honza ran a finger along the spines on the nearest shelf and crossed the room, reading from title to title. *The Middle Pillar… A Suggestive Enquiry… Monas Hieroglyphica…*

The record stopped. The needle muttered until it found the first notes again.

'You were at the luncheon, with Miss Greer.'

Honza startled. He had no recollection of the bell sounding, had not noticed the woman stand beside him, her eyes definitely a deep teak and not black as he had thought in the restaurant.

'You are in anguish.' She excused herself for being so forward.

Honza made no sound. After a moment he nodded.

'It was clear,' she explained, 'at the restaurant. And now.' Her voice was accented, Turkish or something more Eastern still, he did not know. 'Grief and something more.' Neither of them said anything for several moments until she apologised again for being so frank and wondered whether he would like to find somewhere quiet to sit for a time. Honza did not need to hear the voice, prompting, to say yes.

Her name was Elnara. From Turkey, she told him. 'My husband died some while ago and left me a considerable sum. Turkey wishes to modernise and be more European, so a woman may inherit, may use her wealth, may travel. This was not always the case and is not the life of an ordinary woman in my country, or even here. So I give thanks every day for my privilege and devote each day to getting to know the Beloved better, to growing closer to that loving being. God,' Elnara explained. 'In my tradition, we hold that our relationship with the Divine is a deep and passionate love, both our love for the Divine One and the Divine One's love for us.'

The tea rooms bustled everywhere but in this corner. The waitress set the pot gently on the table and withdrew, the crush of wool and gaberdine, the rustle of shopping baskets and chit-chat withdrawing with her.

Honza sipped his tea. He sat back. And felt no need to move or hurry, content with the warmth from the tea.

'You have an interest in magic, mysticism?' Elnara put down her own cup.

'No. Not... exactly. Not until recently...' He tried to keep the explanation short and still it took time to tell of Marietta's search for alchemists and his own for her. 'Rose said she could help.' Honza drained his cup. 'Have you known her long?'

'I do not know her at all. We have a mutual acquaintance and that is how I came to be at the luncheon party.' Elnara shared out the last of the pot.

'Tell me,' she asked after a pause, 'what does your heart say?'

'It was my heart that brought me here.'

'Of course but, in moments of silence, or your dreams, what does it say? About your Marietta, or Miss Greer?'

'I…' Several lines of thought collided and instead of following them Honza found himself trying to justify his actions, make excuses—illness, anxiety… Elnara listened without interrupting and the sour emotion driving the words out of him lessened and fell away. Honza stopped speaking mid-word. He sat back, placing a hand over his mouth, palm sliding down, drawing out the last ire and letting it drip to the floor.

'I have been unwell. And there hasn't been much quiet, not much silence at all.'

Elnara said nothing, letting him continue if he wished.

One of the lines of thought resurfaced: 'Do you not think I should trust Rose?'

'I have met Miss Greer only once, Honza.'

'But in your heart…?'

With a half-smile of acknowledgement, Elnara took a breath. 'There are many paths towards the Beloved but all lead to the same end.'

'Rose says one Art, one Path. Is it different, then, for alchemy?'

'I know very little of alchemy, it is true. And it may be that Miss Greer follows a path that turns and doubles back upon itself and yet still carries a traveller to their destination.'

'Please, you're being obscure. You think I should not trust her?'

'What does your heart say?'

The urge to anger prodded him. Instead of dismissing all this, Honza tried to listen beyond the chatter filling his mind, the exhaustion that still dragged, the feeling of grey dankness that waited and wanted very much to return to him. He listened, searching... and finding...

'I don't know,' he admitted.

'Keep listening,' Elnara advised. 'Do not force an answer. Distrust answers that tell you exactly what you wish to hear, distrust any answer that does not linger. Wait, Honza. Let it come.'

'But I have to— I have to do—'

'A voice can only be heard in silence, so you must listen in—'

'Ah, dear Honza.' Robin's hand fell heavily on Honza's shoulder. 'Been looking all over for you. Miss? Don't think we've had the pleasure.'

'Oh, you were at Rose's luncheon.' The woman with the amethyst broach appeared beside Robin, flanking Honza. Breathless, she fanned her face with her gloves. 'Friend of... oh...'

'How kind of you to remember me.' Elnara stood, motioning Honza to follow. 'We are going to stroll around the museum. Do excuse us.' She took Honza's arm and guided him outside, Robin puffing and ahhing close behind, the woman with the amethyst broach gasping the beginning of an objection and not finding enough breath to finish.

Cold drove fingers deep into Honza's skull as Elnara pulled him out onto the street and across the road towards the British Museum. All too fast. He wanted to pull back. That would mean the others catching up. Head down, he plunged forward through the gates. Directly into someone leaving the museum.

'Steady on, my good fellow, do watch where—'

Honza mumbled an apology, glancing back over his shoulder, gaze passing the man only to return.

'My heavens, Honza Pernath.' Godfrey Howden thrust out his hand. 'Fancy meeting you in this way.'

Robin exclaimed, pulled up short so the woman with the amethyst broach collided with him. Both began to stammer. Godfrey Howden raised an eyebrow. Honza noticed Elnara watching. She waved and started away. He would have called out but Godfrey was apologising.

'Danvers told me you called but I've been deuced busy. You were next on my list, Herr Pernath.' Howden waved Robin and the woman with the amethyst broach into silence. 'Not,' he concluded, 'before time, eh?'

TREMADOG

A CRISP MORNING tramped across the hillsides, talking of winter frosts to come, the shortening days, the sun dipping closer to the horizon. It paused to draw in a deep lungful of air and take in the distant mountains, tops clear of mist, a circling gull crying out to the nearby sea, a crow answering with a single, rough-hewn cry, before adopting silence, a counsel kept.

Honza watched the morning as it strode in scudding cloud, in the slate-dressed breeze ruffling grass and nettle head. He watched the gull cry as it rose, banked, let the day guide it down the hillside, towards the valley and the sea beyond. He watched the crow and the crow, mourning black, settled on the stone wall to watch him, head-tilted and silent. And in the silence, Honza found the urge to paint and draw not so distant, not as far as the village in the valley below the house, or as far as the distant hilltops and mountains, somewhere in the light on the shaggy grass or in the arc of gull and crow, somewhere close enough it was an itch in the fingers, a tingle on the tongue, a tightening of gut and heart, the urge to try and capture just some impression, some essence, of this moment, this sense—

Swinging round, hands thrust deep into jacket pockets and shoulders hunched against the wind and the valley, Honza clenched his teeth. What use painting when the world was the damnable place it was, when people—

The crow barked.

Honza felt his lips curl, bad taste on the tongue. He stomped along the path, slate and granite intermingled, to the patio behind the house. A small table had been set out with breakfast, Honza's plate abandoned, Godfrey Howden's cleared with relish, a second pot of tea resting under a cosy,

Danvers a shadow absorbed into the house. Howden lounged in his chair, a pile of the morning's papers beside his crossed ankles, one crossword dashed off in the time it took him to eat his boiled eggs. Stout brogues, thick wool socks and heavy corduroy trousers, Aran sweater, paisley cravat: Howden looked quite bohemian this morning, unlike his usual spruce and urbane appearance. He propped a book open in his lap, making the occasional pencil note in the margin.

'Anger's a wasteful emotion more often than not. Do try to let go.' Howden glanced up from his book and inclined his head towards the table. 'Have more tea. Or food—Danvers can rustle up fresh feed in no time—but do sit, Honza, and let this go.'

'Easy for you to say,' Honza snapped.

Godfrey Howden turned a page. 'Not actually. It's something I learned with difficulty.' He fixed his gaze on Honza and if there was reproach Honza could find no evidence of it, only a friendly and understanding smile. 'You must feel what you feel but try not to be servant of your feelings. As best you can.'

'I was attacked.' He wanted to sweep the plates off the table. 'Used. Manipulated.'

'Rose went too far, that's true—'

'You're defending her?'

'Not for an instant, dear chap.'

'Then what are you saying?'

Howden's smile did not waver. 'Please, dear fellow, moderate your tone. Let your ire run its course, by all means, but don't let it cloud your opinion of me. Please.'

'I...' Honza blundered passed the table and into the house. 'I apologise.'

'I apologise.'

An hour or so later. Sunlight pitched through the large bow windows at the other end of the study to gild the

Moroccan rugs overlapped across the floor. One window was open, a cool breeze offering the gull's cry.

'I'm being a poor guest.'

Howden was working at his desk at the opposite end of the room from the sweeping windows. 'Not a bit, not a bit.' Howden rounded the desk and opened the study door wider, motioning Honza across the threshold. The desk was an extravagant Art Nouveau affair; between it and the windows the walls were lined with bookshelves, or bookcases with glass doors, any scrap of bare wall hung with pictures and drawings—a small Böcklin, a Redon sketch, a Cézanne, a Masson… chairs, a chaise, chests, book stands and carousels dotted the floor. Despite the breeze the scent of incense lingered.

Godfrey Howden guided him to the window seat.

'I've been a fool.' Honza slumped onto the cushions.

'For accepting an offer of help when you were desperate? A little harsh, old fellow.'

'Then I'm being a fool.'

'Ah well…' Howden laughed. 'We should all wish to be so.' Godfrey leaned across to a low table nearby to sift through a deck of cards resting on it. 'Is the Fool innocent or consciously foolhardy?' Howden held out a card for Honza to take. The illustration showed a blindfolded figure moving along a path leading to a precipice. In one hand, a white rose; in the other, the figure held a red rose. Above the Fool, a black orb floated, a black sun no bigger than the figure's head, a golden sun watching impassively from higher in the sky. Honza peered at the card but could not decide if the figure was male or female.

'The Fool undertakes the journey without being cowed by the prospect of difficulties along the way.' Howden pointed to the card's number. 'No number in some decks, of course, but zero here—in innocence, the Fool has wisdom without knowing it. In mastery, the Fool has wisdom without conceit or pride: the master simply is. Zero appears to have absence at its centre, yet it is a circle encompassing all, empty and full at one and the same time.'

Honza sighed and placed the card back on the cushion beside him. 'I don't understand any of this, not the card, not Rose, not you. Why are you interested in Marietta?'

'I'm not.' Godfrey Howden sat back and crossed his legs. 'Oh, perhaps that's a little sweeping. Your friend is on a curious, wondrous path and I've an interest in such things.'

'But you came to Prague.'

'Yes. An… associate, let's say, was going to be there—to meet, I believe, your Marietta—and I very much wished to speak with him.'

'Your rival? Imogen said—'

'Dear Im, such a flare for the melodramatic.' Godfrey clapped his hands together and laughed. 'We have sometimes been at odds, this associate and I, that's certainly the case, but rivals…?' Howden tapped a thumb against his lips, attention focused inwards. 'A rival suggests we are broadly equals.' He smiled. 'I wouldn't say that was the case.'

Unfurling, Howden leaned forward and patted Honza on the knee before propping elbows on thighs and fixing Honza with an unwavering gaze.

'I wish no harm to your friend, any more than I wish harm to you, Honza. Through the love you feel for this young woman—a very remarkable young woman, unless I miss my mark—you've wandered onto a path you are not prepared for and do not understand. Like the Fool—' Godfrey nodded towards the card— 'you travel in innocence, which is a power but also a vulnerability. There are hazards on the path, failure being the least of them, but there are great bounties, too. Your Marietta follows such a path. It is her own.'

'Rose…' Honza looked out the window—cloudscud, trees in the garden bowing, mountains—seeing only memories. 'Rose said One Art, One Path.'

'So Rose believes. She's mistaken. Truly,' Godfrey added as Honza glanced towards him, confused.

The sun reached through the open window and placed

a hand on his shoulder. Still the tears came. He thought to hide them and abandoned the thought. Howden returned from the desk with a fresh linen handkerchief. Honza blew his nose, the urge to apologise evaporating as he noticed the Fool lying beside him.

'She's lost to me.'

Godfrey Howden spread his hands: *Who can say?*

'But you think I'm on a different path. I can't follow, I can't…'

'One Art, many Paths. All—' Howden picked up the Fool again— 'all may lead to the same end. The Stone, the Elixir: it has many names, as many, almost, as there are paths to it.'

'Lead into gold.' Honza had intended to sound blasé and dismissive but the words came out strangely.

'The mundane into the marvellous, Honza, that's exactly it. And that,' Godfrey Howden emphasised, 'is the Path you have found your way onto.'

Danvers drove them from the house, down into Tremadog, on into Porthmadog, before dropping the saloon car into a lower gear to carry them over the hill into Borth-y-Gest. The tide had retreated, sea into sand, ripples and reflections frozen eddies underfoot as they walked, sun draped in a gauze of pale cloud. A boat roved the horizon beyond the headland, a dog walker churning a diagonal towards the dunes some way off. Otherwise they were alone with the gulls, the distant hiss of the Irish Sea, the grass fringing the beach.

Rose, Godfrey stressed, was not evil, any more than Robin and the woman with the amethyst broach were: 'She follows her own ethical line, not immoral but flexibly amoral.'

She had seen Honza as an opportunity. 'Rather,' Godfrey sighed, 'a shortcut.'

A gull cried out, sending shadows skimming over the sand.

Rose had diverted some of the… 'spiritual flow' Honza had released, without realising, by following Marietta into the Great Work. ('I could talk of *ch'i* or *prana*, or Dr Jung's notions of the libido function, or in terms of the new physics being proposed in Copenhagen and elsewhere, but let's keep it simple, old fellow, and settle on 'spiritual flow' as a shorthand for something subtle, extraordinary, and not actually a jot like spiritualist cant, hm?')

'So they were feeding off me.' Honza paused, wanting the safety of incredulity and not finding it. A memory of the dank presence persisting. 'Like vampires.'

More tonic than sustenance, Godfrey Howden suggested, boosting themselves towards a more heightened state of being. 'Opportunists, as I said.'

And misguided, Howden maintained, because there were no shortcuts. Only the Path and the Work.

The sand grew damper underfoot until they reached the waves and the sea; restive under the moon's influence, each wave hissed as it lapped against the shore and, as they stood in silence, it was easy to imagine each hiss a syllable, each syllable part of a single word, that word apparently incomprehensible, yet that was a distraction to stop the casual listener from attending closely enough, long enough, to begin piecing syllable to syllable and so uncover the first glimmer of comprehension, an understanding that had little to do with syntax and rational thought, word not analysed or atomised, simply… known.

'I can help but I cannot guide.' Howden picked up a length of drift wood and drew in the sand. 'If you wish to continue.'

Honza kept silent.

'I promise nothing.' Howden added a curlicue. 'Except to do what I can.'

Marks in the sand, nothing more.

'Why?'

'Why help you?' Godfrey asked without looking up from his drawing. 'Or why should you go on?'

'Yes. The latter.' Honza folded his arms. 'Both.'

'Oh.' Godfrey Howden paused to admire his work. 'Reasons. My own. A little altruism. Rather more selfish curiosity. Other reasons. As to the second question…' He leaned, so as not to mark the sand, and added a final stroke.

'As to that: you cannot know what wonders await at the end of the Path, what marvels. In continuing, there is no saying which other Paths you might cross. Or who might return to you along the way.'

Just marks in the sand.

I'll think about it.

They had talked about art over dinner, and music. Godfrey spoke of meeting Kandinsky and Ernst, Stravinsky and Louis Armstrong. He spoke of how much he admired Honza's painting, its mix of the abstract and concrete, the pastoral and urban, showing them not as dualities but aspects of an unexpressed quality linking them: there was much, Howden emphasised, much of the spirit, of the soul, in Honza's work.

Honza had been unable to respond, emotion welling and setting his hands trembling. He sat back, head bowed to hide his face, keeping silent while Godfrey continued to speak of music, his travels, words reassuring, neither prodding him out of his mood nor forcing him deeper.

At the end of the meal, Honza excused himself, Godfrey Howden telling him there was no reason to apologise for his conduct or emotions. You have, Howden told him, a lot to think on.

I'll think about it.

The mountains peered at him through the window,

even with the curtains closed and the bedside lamp turned off.

Marram grass whispered.

What's to think on? a voice asked.

'I told him I would.'

That's not what I mean. The voice moved away through the night and Honza climbed from under the covers. The dining table stood at the foot of the bed, his own food untouched, three courses lined up, side by side; of Howden's dinner there was only crumbs, a smear of sauce, black against the night.

'How come I can see?'

Don't change the subject.

Marram grass whispered and the tide was rising again, erasing each footprint and mark.

She won't come, the voice reminded him.

'Shut up.'

It's not like you have a choice, the voice continued and the voice might have been the rising tide, or the mountains, or the wind through the marram grass, but was none of those things.

You blame yourself.

Dark hair, dark skin. No hint of red, only jet. First light of the rising moon.

'They took from me. Blood. And not just blood.' Honza hoped the mountains would agree with him. But they had turned away, leaving dunes, marram, shore running into the sea. A short step and shallow at that.

The water frightened him.

Is that what you deserved?

'I didn't ask for this,' Honza raged, kicking away the last of the mark in the sand before the sea had chance to reach it. With each kick, the moon pulled blackness about itself until there was only an inky sphere above the waves. Jet against the night. The man, all black, held out a hand, a star, small and feeble, in his palm.

She will not come.

And the man, all black, pointed with his other hand.

She let the shallow slope carry her away from the shore, further inland, the black sun setting over the waves. It sank. Soundless and without ripple.

'I didn't ask for this,' Honza yelled. 'I was happy. I had prospects. Admirers. Not just amateur collectors but respected critics, collectors willing to pay real money. I was—' He gasped, feet skating over the sand, he was running so fast, rage driving him down the beach. 'I was—'

Throat closed, tight, voice lost somewhere. He could no longer speak.

Sand gave way to rocks, rocks plunging beneath the surface and the sea hissing, hissing.

Honza threw himself backwards.

'I didn't ask for any of this.'

The shoreline was deserted, dunes likewise. No one was listening. Even Honza was unsure who had spoken.

He woke up crying, grief doubling him over, hands clawing at the mattress, trying, blindly, to dig to another world where she had not gone, had stayed, a world where—

Fresh tears, body growing rigid, knotted with wishes... with wishing... wishing...

But there was no picking the thoughts apart. All there was were tears and grief and, somewhere between, a quiet space where there were no emotions.

Or more than anyone could feel.

They took packed lunches and thermos flasks, a haversack each, Danvers driving them a few miles further along the Llyn Peninsula before motoring in the direction of Bangor with instructions to meet them later that afternoon.

'You might find this interesting,' was all Godfrey Howden said as they set off along narrow lanes, before tramping over several fields to a rough pathway of stone.

Across a small bridge a ruin waited, walls of an old house, granite blocks weathered and mottled with lichen, roof not even a memory. Water nattered to itself as it dashed away along a channel that seemed to come out of the ruin itself.

'This is Ffynnon Gybi,' Howden explained, 'St Cybi's Well. Cybi was a Cornish saint, one of the ancient Celtic variety.'

Honza rested a hand on the weathered granite. This was all 18th Century, Godfrey explained, a building for the well, one for the well keeper. Honza closed his eyes, concentrating on rock shaped by hundreds of summers and winters, by wind and rain.

'Of course,' Godfrey shrugged, 'this place would have been in use before St Cybi loaned his name to the well, long before Celtic Christians came here.'

Not reaching for an image or a single impression, Honza waited for whatever might come.

He saw Marietta's face and snatched his hand away.

Howden beckoned him forward. 'Here.'

Inside, a large pool, stone flagged, stone lined.

'It's...' Honza swallowed, hollowness reforming in the pit of his throat, limbs heavy as fresh tears prickled. This grief should be passed by now, he thought. 'It's very... tranquil.'

His hand smarted.

The surface of the well caught the sky without a ripple, grey clouds hiding the base of the cistern beneath their reflections, his own reflection little more than a silhouette. A breeze set the long grass to muttering, oak, rowan and elder, murmuring back.

Godfrey unshouldered his haversack, tugging up the sleeve of his tweed jacket as he settled beside the cistern.

'Wells are liminal, not quite of this world nor of the world beyond.' He trailed a finger across the water.

Honza watched, ripples spreading, overlapping. He thought of several replies, each of them too flip, without insight. He wondered if this was why Marietta had left, that at heart he was as soulless as Karel.

'They offer cures, a place of divination, a place of prayer.' Howden drew another line across the surface. 'Sit down, Honza,' Godfrey suggested, 'you'll see better.'

'What world? Beyond, I mean.'

'Oh. For the Celts it would have been the Otherworld, the place of ancestors, of the færy. For others, it might be the *Mundus Imaginalis*, or the world of archetypes. Call it the Collective Unconscious, if you like.'

'I don't understand.' It felt like the first true thing he had said in weeks.

Another line, ripples brimming, mingling. 'I think you do,' Godfrey Howden said, sitting back to wait for the ripples to settle.

Honza saw the water still, become a mirror once more, a breeze drawing breath as it clambered up the sides of the ruin to peered over the wall. The well remained untroubled, holding Honza's reflection unchanging, silhouette motionless against the drift of cloud, grey on grey, the only sign that time still passed. Minutes of time. Or hours, a clutch of days perhaps passing before Godfrey Howden asked:

'How do you feel?'

His voice was soft enough to have been the breeze, or the grass, or the branches on an elder tree.

'Broken.' Honza's voice was only a little louder.

'And when you dream?'

'I don't dream.'

The water grew still, stillness spreading, weathered stones of the old house embracing the stillness, their thoughts slow by nature, slow and ordered along interstice and crystal margin, memories long, the flitter come-and-go of people, their words and names, barely registering at all. Images not words lingered, images instead of a dozen breathless thoughts...

'And when you dream?'

'I don't...'

The stillness. Winding itself around the walls, up through the branches of the trees nearby. Eyes obsidian, no surface sheen only depth, infinite, a black that absorbed all light, all words. Only the image remained, beyond words: scales black and twined around trees and walls, tail stirring the clouds.

'I don't know who they are.'

'Don't let that be a worry. It is no worry. Nothing of consequence, Honza.'

'Oh.'

Word more a thought than a sound. Godfrey Howden understood, even so, and asked Honza to describe the figures in the dream, the old man, the dark-haired man, the woman only seen at a distance. And Honza found himself telling the story of the angel in the gallery, the two dragons beneath the black sun, the stillness slowing his heart, leaving time between beats for the words to find their way to the well water and slip beneath the surface, slip out of sound into image, into memory, into...

'Yes.'

The stones became silent. The trees folded their branches, bowed their heads. And the stillness, the stillness grew wings and made the wings into a sky, a night sky flecked with stars, stars smoky quartz and almost invisible amongst the clouds.

'Yes.' Godfrey sat back from the well. 'The man with dark hair is trying to divert you.'

Honza looked at the black figure in the well. 'She will not come.'

'That remains to be seen,' Godfrey Howden announced, dragging two fingers across the water. A crow gave a long cry that flapped away into the trees, setting the branches swaying. A leaf settled in the middle of Honza's reflection.

Call it a trance, Godfrey explained as they searched for a spot to eat lunch.

'I would have asked permission, dear fellow, but there are blocks within you I wanted to circumvent. The man,' Howden explained, 'the man with dark-coloured hair.'

They made do with a stretch of verge. Steam rose as each thermos was uncorked.

'This figure bars your progress.' Godfrey bit into a sandwich. 'He might be explained in psychological terms as easily as spiritual ones but the result is the same: you must overcome his resistance, find a way for the dark-hair man to let you pass. Only this will bring the desired results.

'Assuming,' he added after sipping tea, 'you wish to continue along the path you have begun, Honza?'

Honza remembered the stillness, flowing from well water to stone block.

'I wish I could go back and be the person I was before I met her.'

Howden silently acknowledged this wish.

The beaker of tea in his hands cooled. There was an edge to the air. They were only a handful of kilometres from the sea, Honza thought, turning his face to the wind. And the wind touched his face, brushed at the tears so the tears cooled against his skin.

'Nothing could be the same. I've experienced things. I've felt pain I never felt before, grief…'

A crow drew breath, spoke once. Honza searched the hedgerow, the oaks and hollies along the vergeside, without finding the bird. Only it's voice and that had gone away almost before he knew it was there.

'And so you feel broken,' Godfrey murmured, holding out the handkerchief from his breast pocket.

Honza wiped his eyes. A tractor coughed and hawked, maundering into life, sound carrying over several fields. The crow remained silent and the wind retreated from the noise.

'I think,' Godfrey began, measuring each word for suitability and merit, 'I think that if you tried to go back, the sense of dissatisfaction would overwhelm you, dear fellow. You would be all the more broken.'

'But—' The pain of his heart was crushing, words clotting in his throat, pain harrowing each nerve, each muscle and bone. In the distance, the tractor coughed and complained. And a motorcar slouched passed, gears rasping. Oblivious. Some things in the world remained oblivious to the harrowing and the pain. Only the clouds grew still and bowed their heads.

'She won't come,' he admitted, no longer able to think otherwise.

They walked on, tractor's grizzle and grump trying to follow and getting tangled in a blackthorn thicket, lanes made quiet for the calling of pigeon, sparrow natter, the rustle of blackbirds in the undergrowth, of things unseen nosing beneath holly bushes, hedges otherwise turning bare and brittle at the sight of coming winter.

The stones hunkered in the unclaimed space between criss-crossing boundary walls. As they tramped over the last field, the capstone drew a line across the distant hills.

Arthur's Quoit was one name for the dolmen, Godfrey Howden said, spreading his hands across the capstone so that it looked more stone altar than burial chamber roof. '*Ystum Cegid Isaf*, in Welsh,' Godfrey added, head bowed.

A hush circled the dolmen. The air smelled of damp leaves, of winter waiting over the horizon, not far, not long.

Honza turned to retrace their path. He had seen enough.

'Get inside.'

Pretend this is a joke, Honza cautioned himself, a mistake. Pretend something.

'Please, Honza: get inside.'

Howden held a hand towards the space beneath the capstone, between uprights so tapered no imagination was needed to foresee them toppling at the slightest push.

'Honza, please.'

Hand of invitation, not compulsion. Honza dropped

his haversack, not meeting Howden's gaze as he crawled between the uprights.

'Lie down.' Godfrey Howden knelt to peer beneath the stone roof, finger tracing shapes on the air.

Only shapes.

Honza lay on his back. In the place where a dead king had lain.

'Just so, a dead king,' Godfrey Howden agreed and Honza guessed he had spoken aloud, grew more self-conscious, cool of the earth leaching through his clothes, a nerve in one thigh jumping.

'To move forward, the old king must die.' Godfrey Howden placed a palm flat on the grass, rested the other on the capstone. 'You must die to yourself and come to a new life with the rising of the king.'

Asking what all that meant felt like so much effort that Honza lay back against the cold ground, uprights marking the day off into sections: a glimpse of cloud, stalled mid-sky, a hillside distant and gravid, grass stalks closer by.

Honza closed his eyes when he was told. Earth unyielding, cold against shoulders and skull.

'Don't say anything,' Godfrey cautioned. 'Simply observe. Simply be: in this moment, in this body.'

Unyielding. Chill, seeping. Also the sound of air moving. Of the open chamber, stones rooted deep. Part of the earth. As the earth formed a part with the sky. And Honza, lying against grass and cool earth, shoulders, pelvis, calves, heels. Muscles tensed. Consciously trying to relax. Blood's pulse in his ears. A bruise on his knee, pain small and unnoticed until this moment, pain growing under the touch of his attention. Mind straying. Cold days. Praha, cold days in Praha. Her face. Her voice. And conversations that should have gone differently, rewritten along with reviews of exhibitions, or exhibitions that never had been but might, might, might have been her face reflected in a window or, or— Thoughts came and went, memories more present than his body and these stones and this earth and the light of cloud and sun and the cry of a crow, rooks in the distance, something just outside the open-sided chamber, on the opposite side of the dolmen from where Godfrey Howden knelt—'These thoughts have no weight, let them go. The you that watches, worries over past and future, has no weight. Let it go, let it...' Only emptiness beneath the chatter. A silence of muscle, joint, one eyelid's twitch, tension across the forehead... And each might be the earth, the stones, the day...

Something waited outside the dolmen.

Only silence beneath the chatter.

Something. A shape in the dusk, indistinct, close but insubstantial. A word. A gesture. Something hunkered beside the dolmen, blocking the view between the upright stones. As it should be, as it should—cold earth unyielding, space closed off, a word, a gesture. A mark in the earth, in the sand. 'Don't.'

Godfrey's voice, in the chamber beside him.

'Don't allow it. Look.'

Only dusk. Only chamber, hunkered, blocking the view between here and a someone in the near distance. Beckoning (a gesture), speaking (a word), voice indistinct in the dusk. Clench of muscle and breath and throat tight, figure (dark) leaning through the uprights (blocking), the dusk, the sky, unchanged, a hand, outstretched, a shape in the dusk (dark), waving him (the sand) back, back from the opening (the shore), a mark in the sand, an outstretched hand (blocking) framing something in the dusk, waving (towards the shore, the tide coming out of the night, the darkness, across the sand, erasing), beckoning, beyond the outstretching hand (in the darkness).

Honza turned on his side, drawing knees to chest, eyes squeezed shut, muscles straining until, little by little, there was earth below and stone above. And only silence beneath the chatter.

There were canvases and paints, sketch books and charcoal, a host of sundries, set out in the sitting room when they returned.

'I want you to paint,' Godfrey told Honza. 'I want you to draw and sketch.'

'I don't want to.' A headache graved itself into his skull, muscles weak with fatigue. Honza took another step backwards and collided with Danvers.

'Is everything to your satisfaction, sir?' The grey-haired man bowed as he spoke.

'No.' Word almost a shout.

'Wonderful,' Godfrey announced, it was all wonderful. 'Thank you so much, Danvers.' Howden beamed as Danvers bowed again and closed the door behind him.

The headache wound tightly across both eyes. 'I don't paint any more.' Honza failed to keep his voice level and repeated his words more loudly, panic shooing him away from the artist's materials until his shoulders struck the closed door.

'And I sympathise,' Godfrey replied, smile not altering to any degree. 'But I want—I need you to paint her.'

Honza knew his mouth was hanging open, both fists aching they were clenched so tightly. There was no way to relax and the tremor in his muscles intensified.

'Yes.' Howden took a step closer, another. 'Yes, old fellow. I know the pain. I see the fear—'

'I'm not—' Honza swallowed. Tasting acid, the taste of copper filling his mouth. 'I'm not— Not frightened.'

'And still I ask a lot. I promise nothing except to do what I can, Honza. I don't ask this of you lightly.' Godfrey Howden rested a hand on Honza's shoulder. 'You have no reason to trust and experience encourages suspicion.'

Knees giving way, Honza managed to get to the sofa with Godfrey's help, thigh barking against the armrest as he slumped over the cushions. 'Today,' he mumbled.

'Of course, of course. Insensitive of me and I do apologise, old fellow, forgive me.' Godfrey sat on the coffee table. 'Hot tea. And a good, stiff brandy, after a bath. Danvers will do you something restorative on a tray. Please, old fellow, I simply sensed a desire in you to push on.'

A passing impression, of someone just behind his shoulder, someone else beside the window. No sunset, dusk crawling into night and night creeping around the house, talking in the voice of a tawny owl, in the barking of a fox. There was a smell, fire not lit in the hearth to keep it away, smell of mist, the earth and rock beneath turning cold. Honza stirred and eventually managed to meet Howden's gaze.

'I'm—'

'Do not apologise, Honza. I've overstepped the bounds, dear fellow. You're all in and it's deuced chilly in here, too cold to chat, so—'

'Why?' He sat up, clinging to the arm of the sofa. The night grew limbs, tenuous fingers brushing against the glass, curtains yet to be drawn. 'Why paint Marietta?'

'As focus.' Godfrey's voice was hushed, bonhomie and concern become a quiet intensity. He watched Honza, unblinking, so Honza forgot about the night and the cold and the impressions that had nothing to do with exhaustion. 'A focus for you. Change requires will. Will requires focus. You must know her again, as if, by the merest whim, you might conjure her presence, here, in this very house, Honza, conjure her physical, living presence. The tone of her voice. The tension in the muscles of her mouth when she laughed. The warmth and texture of her skin.'

'You understand.'

Honza nodded.

Finding his throat was dry, he swallowed. 'Yes. But… why?'

'Her path became your path as your path has become its own, and that way will only open if you draw deeper and yet deeper on your imagination. Marietta's image carries power for you. That power is invaluable.

'Now—' Godfrey Howden sat back, hands clasped

together. 'Let's get you that bath, that tea, and that brandy, eh?'

In the darkness, the glowing wristwatch dial showed it was not yet seven. Honza stretched and yawned, more rested than he had felt in weeks. Impulse pushed him out of bed and into his clothes, stairs creaking, a light under the kitchen door suggesting Danvers at least was also up and about.

East stained grey, west swallowing mist and hilltops, night not yet ready to leave. Honza shrugged deeper into his overcoat and followed the path to the end of the garden, each step uncertain on the damp flagstones. A hedge ran along the boundary, broken by a drystone wall, itself interrupted by a wooden gate leading out onto the hillside. Biting his lip, wary of loosing his balance, Honza clambered onto the wall and faced eastwards.

Birds sang, calling across a landscape not yet solid but still hazed in smudged tones, a ghostly indigo spilling from some areas yet to gain definition with the gathering dawn. The breeze had smoke on its breath, a bur of coal fires from the village below where a few lights showed.

Honza closed his eyes. Listened. To his heart, the rustle of his clothes. The birds, the sough of the light wind chivying the mist. Deep breath, chilled and damp on the tongue. The feel of the stones through his shoes.

The wind sighed. And grew still.
The birds sighed. And grew still.
The village was silent.
Only the hillside moved, settling itself, deeper, down to the bedrock far beneath his feet.

Opening his eyes, Honza looked towards clouds pale with the sun's approach.

'Honza...'

He tried not to think of the day before, the whole day oddly vague, more figment, dream fragment. He tried not to think.

'Honza, do be careful.'

It was perceptible. If he stood and let each thought slip away, words passing without leaving a mark, without trying to retell pasts or rehearse futures… if he let these thoughts be marks in the sand, tide smoothing them away, no trace… if he did that then it was perceptible: the coming of the dawn, beyond the mist and the cloud.

'Honza, don't miss your step.'

The hills merged into the mist, a gull motionless, wings part of the mist, mist and the passing night, night the only shadow, the only silhouette.

'Honza—'

Silhouette a part of yesterday, forgotten like his dreams, only a good night's rest, only night coming into day.

'Honza, you must—'

Each hilltop bowed, remembering times long past when they had no name, memories nothing but dim images and yet each image a story, each story rooted into the deep earth where time ran at its own pace. Where there was no time. Only now: sunrise. Honza wanted to bow to the hills and the mountains, wanted to creep as glaciers crept or flame as molten magma flamed, watch one north star lose grip of the pole and fall away to leave a void and see that void gradually, gradually filled by another star that, one day, would slip away too. Leaving sunrise, sunset. Leaving old instincts to bellow in glee as they found themselves running across escarpment and peak, instincts ancient and huge, part the passing of seasons and part the stories of gods and stars and glacial hillsides and images of dreams and visions, visions of the land being shaped and stars being moved and the passing of weather and the turning of leaf and a budding and a dying back to bud again, heavens mirroring the sweep of days. To sunset. Sunrise.

'You must be careful, Honza, you must listen—'

A moment's glimmer before the mist closed, transmuting gold into pewter.

Honza gasped, foot skidding on the stones, keeping his

balance as he watched grey-blue light spread across the hillsides. No memory of a presence beside his shoulder. Only the course of adrenaline. Only the image, lingering until he reached the house and then lost: clouds parting to offer a flare of gold, before the mist plucked away the dawn-sun's veil to reveal the blackened face beneath.

Muscles unused and unpracticed, each mark and gesture stiff, uncoordinated. Yet by mid-afternoon when Godfrey came to ask if he cared for a walk, there were two or three decent sketches amongst the sheets torn from the pad, and many more studies in the sketch book that at least began to capture… something of Marietta. She was still lost and distant but Honza accepted that she was also still very much present, a part of him.

It seemed a poor substitute.

'And yet she is here, even if in so limited a sense,' Howden observed as they scrambled over a field gate and angled up a sweeping hillside. The sky closed tightly over the mountain tops, horizon pulled in to form the walls of a grey flask enclosing the house and the hill it sat upon: reach out far enough and you would be sure to brush fingers tips against the walls of the vessel.

They paused at an outcrop. Dank air chill on his face as Honza foundered over the right words to to tell Godfrey about the vision at sunrise.

'These things have the power of image and that power transcends words, which are clumsy things.' Godfrey Howden leaned against the outcrop of rocks, hands pushed deep into the pockets of his tweed jacket, ankles crossed. He gazed across the width of this flask of mist and cloud, granite and sod.

'Still I wish I could explain it better.' Honza paced out a few steps, turned back to the rock, paced out again, restless. 'Do you think it mad?'

'Quite the opposite, dear fellow. This—' Godfrey

beckoned, patting the weathered rock beneath him. 'This is deeply rooted, you would say?'

Honza nodded. The stone drew heat from his palm. He shivered and felt unexpectedly invigorated.

'The impression is that mind and body are separate,' Howden continued, spreading his own fingers across the granite. 'Descartes was grossly mistaken. But so are some mystics. Mind is rooted deeply in body.' He tapped the rock. 'As body is rooted deeply in mind. We are neither the ethereal beings some mystics would advocate, nor are we the roughcast some Gnostics abjure. We are something of both and yet a little of neither. There are vistas inside and out, Honza, and this is the journey you are on—exploring this terrain that lies between the false dualisms of Mind and Body, Matter and Spirit…'

The rock felt like any other rock. The day felt closed in and the flash of invigoration was spent and gone. Grass slick underfoot, the step back from the outcrop threatened to become slip and fall. Anger flashed, beneath ribs and sternum, heating acid and bile until they frothed.

'I heard a voice.'

He struggled to remain calm.

'A voice saying my name.'

'And you ignored it?' Godfrey Howden asked softly, leaning forward until he had Honza's attention.

'Yes.'

That, Godfrey Howden told him, was a good thing. And when Honza asked if he was going mad, Godfrey Howden assured him this was not so.

You must root yourself, Honza, was Howden's advice. In your painting, mind and body as one, Godfrey told him and Honza said yes, unsure where the anger had come from, feeling confused but saying yes again.

Danvers brought him tea that evening.

The bedroom was littered with sketches, some

abandoned before they had quite begun, others pursued until they were run down or lost in the chase.

'I should advise drinking your nightcap while still hot, sir.' Danvers's expression did not flicker at the chaos gripping the room.

Honza sniffed. Found mint, found camomile. A bitterness beneath. 'What's in this?'

'Herbs, sir. Mr Howden's creation.' Danvers retreated to the door as Honza took a first sip. 'And, sir, if I may venture to observe, I believe you are trying too hard in your endeavours. If my understanding is correct, a degree of relaxation aids the creative flow.'

The door closed softly.

For a moment he felt sure he had thrown the tea cup after Danvers, so clear was the impression of tea spattering the door, the clatter of broken crockery. Honza struggled to slow his breathing, knowing Danvers was right and hating the man for making him acknowledge this fixated rush was not the way to create the painting he was beginning to see.

Honza drained the cup. He felt foolish, angry at his own anger and more foolish for that. The tea made a molten line down his throat, a pool of fire spreading, warmth easing knots of tension from his neck, a headache he had barely noticed loosening. His knees and shoulders ached, muscles tight for too long. Honza had been pushing too greatly.

He felt a fool. And remembered what Godfrey had said about fools.

No dreams that night, sleep untroubled and enclosing, more restful than the night before.

Honza rose before dawn and walked to the end of the garden to watch the sunrise. Rain closed off the horizon, hiding the sun but unable to snuff out its light. Honza could make out a slight cup on the horizon, the point where the sun rose, was rising behind the walls of cloud, its light making the raincloud gleam, become glowing shadow. Not a cup: a mouth, a mouth giving voice to the morning sun. Honza heard it speak the sun and the mouth in the hillside spoke with Marietta's voice, spoke Marietta's name.

The mundane into the marvellous, Honza thought. And that thought had her voice, too.

He sketched. He made studies. Unaware of anything else, not the hills nor the passage of sun or weather, certainly unaware of voices because Godfrey had to speak several times before he broke through, Godfrey speaking to suggest using another room, having use of a room at the back of the house, beneath the bow-windowed study, room very nearly round itself, easily cleared and likely to make a more suitable studio than this bedroom, Honza taking a few moments to understand, much less than that to agree. He remembered to thank Danvers for the advice of the other evening, too, and in passing he asked about the faint smell in the round room and Danvers thought, perhaps, incense had been burned in there for some soiree or other although he could not recollect the event clearly. And Honza accepted an offer of herb tea as readily as he accepted the studio, the lingering scents of frankincense, amber and sandalwood, and began work. I might paint soon, he told Godfrey Howden later that day and, only as he did, realising how late it was. I forgot to eat, Honza remarked, not feeling hungry at all and Godfrey Howden observed that fasting was good for the soul. And by then night had overtaken the studio and there was a little supper and a hot tea nightcap and sleep deep as the night was deep as the rocks were rooted, sleep apparently unbroken by any dreams other than dreams of Marietta, any other voices than Marietta's, any word other than her name bringing the next sunrise.

Pallet knife and broad brush, the first three canvases came quickly, finding space in the round studio beside rough sketches and more detailed studies.

Danvers was despatched to Manchester for more supplies. At my expense, Godfrey Howden insisted. Honza felt shame mix with pride. And put both aside to begin another painting.

He felt Marietta beside him in the round studio. Is that ridiculous? he asked, nodding to the empty stool positioned to get the best of the smudged-charcoal light that was all the cloud-capped days seemed to offer.

Do you feel her coming closer? Godfrey Howden asked, regarding the stool with an unreadable expression.

I see her sitting there, when I paint, Honza replied, stretching fresh canvas across a frame. I hear Marietta talk to me when I speak to her.

Capital, Godfrey Howden murmured.

Another painting took shape: Marietta walking along the side of a road, the landscape alive with old gods and yet older stories, the sun a ruby overhead. Honza heard insects as he put in further details, felt a breeze, warm and scented, play across his hands. The warmth made the paint dry more quickly than expected. Honza spoke to himself as he worked, not hearing the words, not sure later if there had been words spoken aloud or if they had been part of the painting after all.

Danvers brought herb teas, fruit. Honza was hardly eating. Fasting was good for the soul.

In the late afternoon, as shadows began to crouch under the tables and the day slipped out of its robes to reveal the night beneath, Honza went down to the bottom of the garden, climbed the stone wall and turned towards the mountain tops, mist obscuring the village below and leaving the house alone inside curved walls of hillside and changing mist. Honza watched, unsure if the last glimmer of light had fallen away. One peak marked a point as close to due west as he could guess, peak hard to find in this mist. He searched, imagining the sun climbing down its side, beyond ground level and on into some underworld where it would walk deep corridors, through vast caverns, until the mouth of the east could speak it in the dawning of another day.

There were people missing from the canvas.

Honza pointed to the space on either side of Marietta as she walked along a dusty, southern road.

She has, he explained, companions.

Godfrey Howden stood motionless. Indeed, was all he said, before clapping Honza on the shoulder and telling him he was doing capital work, capital.

Tell me, Godfrey asked, pausing at the doorway, do you dream still?

Of Marietta. Honza dreamed of her but had no other dreams, none that he remembered. Why?

Capital work, Godfrey Howden told him, stepping aside to allow in Danvers, tea pot and a selection of fruit on a tray.

The smell of incense was stronger.

Halos of paint walked beside Marietta, original underpainting wiped away to reveal the canvas at the centre of each smear.

Honza stood back. Glanced towards the stool. And frowned, aware that it was empty, would always remain so.

Snatching up a tube of paint, mixing pigments with stiff, jagged thrusts of the brush, tightness returning to neck and shoulders as he tried to shake the mood. Brush freezing over the smeared halos, unable to bring paint to canvas.

He could see her companions. Not clearly. Not as clearly. But—

The brush shook.

Later, towards the end of the afternoon, Godfrey Howden came in, to find the ruby sun more fully realised and a fine network of lines, almost like threads spun by a gilded spider, crisscrossing the landscape, tiny symbols marking each one, sometimes astrological, sometimes obscure, symbols clustering close to Marietta and the smears where the paint had been cleared away and cleared away and cleared from her companions.

Honza did not look up when Godfrey asked about the waiting spaces. Taking another sheet of paper and beginning another sketch, all Honza would say was: They'll come later.

Several dozen new drawings scattered the round studio's floor when Danvers knocked and announced that supper was served. Honza said he would be right along.

Sometime later, Godfrey came in. 'I'm waiting on you, dear fellow.' Howden's tone was mild. 'Won't you join me?'

Hiding resentment at the interruption, Honza followed Howden into the dining room.

'How is the painting coming along?'

'Fine.' Vegetables steamed in a serving dish. Honza felt unexpectedly hungry.

'You're not starting on something else, are you? Those sketches…?'

'Another idea,' Honza mumbled, chewing. 'Is there any more?' Danvers deferred to Godfrey, who reminded Honza he had eaten very little of late. He should treat his digestion lightly—perhaps a little fruit?

Thinking better of replying, Honza took a pear from the bowl Danvers held out, reminding himself Godfrey was right and he should be ashamed at the vehemence of his reaction. No, he thought, finishing the pear, more confused than ashamed—

'But you're not abandoning the painting?'

Godfrey sounded casual, attention on his own plate.

'Don't know. The composition's—' He could see them as he spoke, the companions walking beside Marietta. They nodded to him and seemed comfortable in his presence but they refused the journey from imagination to nerve impulse to the fine workings of muscle and paint brush.

'Oh, please, dear fellow, it's an extraordinary painting, much one of the best I've seen from you. You simply must finish it,' Godfrey Howden rested elbows on table, chin on clasped hands, mouth hidden so there were only his eyes, blue ice shards catching the light.

'I—'

'Dear fellow,' Godfrey Howden murmured, 'I insist. You simply must.'

This is how days passed inside the flask of hillside and cloud: companions taking form only to slip away, a drift of mist on the tip of a brushstroke. Gone from reach in moments. So there was rag and wiping and underpainting anew. A fresh line for shoulder, for head, for eyes: sometimes an owl, sometimes a star come to earth. Sometimes. More often mist. They will not form, he raged and Howden, dear Howden, offered sympathy, and tea, and another plea that this canvas not, not be abandoned.

Days passed this way. And evenings…

Sepia pencil. Lines echoing the arcana of Rembrandt or da Vinci. A low headland that lay close to the sea, land sinuous, alive under the sea's touch, their embrace so ardent land was part of sea as sea was inseparable from earth and rock. In some there was a house, set on a rise above the tideline or further back at the foot of the hill rising to form a low mountain, but the house always a thing drawn forth from the land, its windows fixed on the horizon, watching each wave, each weather front unfolding. Neither chimney smoke nor candle flicker, the house appearing empty and yet, in shading, the flex of pencil line, a sense lingered of a thing alive unto itself and empty only in the sense that its occupant had stepped out, somewhere on the island. In others, the ruins of an old church; or the foothills of the mountain; or the cliffs, away from the low headland, black rocks washed with spume and where seals basked, merpeople at home as much in air as in the rise and fall of the seas, so long as their skins remained wet. But in each, and in the others that followed, the hint of a figure, barely a suggestion in some, a dark shape in others. Never quite seen, albeit recognised from countless dreams; standing, sometimes, often seen on the verge of turning, perhaps even speaking.

The sketches spilled from the table as he moved. Sleeper waking, disorientation making the room a stranger, making the pencil in his hand someone else's, as surely as the hand must belong elsewhere. This evening: a drawing of a stretch of path around the island, deserted but for the shadows cast by clouds drifting towards the central mountain; and another of the shore, deserted it seemed until, with a start, he picked out the figure on the far side of the shallow bay, not back-turned but facing out of the sketch. Only a handful of pencil marks, nothing more. And yet. Honza could not shake the conviction that the figure was signalling. No one else in the picture. Except, in a sense, himself, viewing this sweep of sea and island from some point just beyond the edges of the sheet of paper.

Some point, he knew with certainty, near the cottage.

A knock at the door. Danvers' voice.

'One, er, one moment, uh, please, Mr Danvers, I'm—er—almost dressed.' Snatching open the bedroom door and wiping away an attempt at a cheerful smile in the same instant, sure such a display of high spirit would arouse suspicion and unsure why that should matter as he said, 'Yes, Mr Danvers?'

'Mr Howden wonders if you would care to take tea with him, sir.'

Of course Honza would. He would be along in just a moment, he assured Danvers, part of him watching Danvers's gaze flicker away—over Honza's shoulder, across the room, to rest on the table, pencils, paper—and back again, as another part of him questioned why Danvers should be anything other than curious.

Closing the door, Honza slipped the large portfolio out from under the pile of sketch pads on the dressing table and looked at the collected sepia drawings. Well over a dozen in the last few days. And no conscious memory of having drawn any of them.

Darkness stoppered the flask until Marietta spoke to the awakening sun the following dawn. Each evening there was talk, in the sitting room or the half-moon study, or more often in the round studio where the smell of incense waxed, never waned, where Godfrey Howden had installed offerings from other parts of the house, to help, he declared with each addition, the creative process. So amongst studies and canvases, an iron bust of Saturn, in the form of the Titan, Kronos, unpicking the hands of a clock, time a myth and gods banishing the trivial flitter of calendar pages and train timetables; and opposite, a statuette of Pan, by the same hand as Kronos but wrought in bronze, the goat-foot god, priapic and lustful, with hands plunged into the earth as if wishing to halt the turning of the world, or perhaps drag Gaia into torrid clinch; and to complete a trinity, a copper plaque of the sun, crafted by a different hand, sun's brow crowned with briars and nightshade flowers, face beatific in some lights and yet strangely vacant from other angles, as if conscious thought had given way to sensation and being, simply being. Admiring of its artisanship though he was, Honza let his attention stray to this third piece least of all, even though Godfrey Howden seemed most pleased the plaque had found a place in this room, this circular room that smelled of incense and where they sat and talked often in the evenings in the stoppered flask of hills and mist.

Godfrey spoke of art and of music, of course, a collector of books and *objects d'art* and scores autographed by the composer, a connoisseur of these things, and Honza found himself captivated, smells of pigment, smells of incense mingling with herb tea, a distant trace of mist and hillside and darkness, room silent but for words, for voice, but for art and music and the sound of a voice, night paused to listen as Honza listened, until there was no thought of thoughts, of things done or to do. Only Godfrey's voice. Music. The arts. Places been and people met. Music, art.

The Art.

In fragments at first, by omission as much as reference. And Honza listened, words not passing over him as the next sip of tea soothed him that little closer to sleep.

Astrum in homine, Godfrey said, seeming mesmerised by his own words. And Honza sat a fraction straighter, although the tea lulled and the night grew still around the hour when he should go to sleep if he was to meet the sunrise tomorrow.

Think of Shelley's rose…

Godfrey held up his hand and his fingers might well have curled around the stem of a rose.

… flower sheltered within the furl of its own leaves. It is all around us but we miss it as easily as a flower hidden within its own leaves.

Godfrey let the flower fall.

But there are ways, he added and closed his mouth and looked at nothing in the room that Honza could see, his eyelids heavy and an itch of tiredness invading muscle and bone.

It goes well, the canvas?

It goes slowly.

Always the same answer, followed by good nights exchanged and good wishes for a restful sleep and the muse's blessing come the new day.

Evenings passed this way. And nights…

Wakefulness lapped around the bed, a neap tide lifting him out of sleep, beached, blinking at shapes half-formed around the room, paddling back towards shallows and deep sleep beyond, and being carried back to consciousness, thoughts stirring, forming lines, dialogues that anchored him to the bed, to the room in darkness, to attempts at reiterating parts of the day gone by, or shaping a day yet to come.

Each night much the same. A few hours sleep, black and depthless and, it seemed, untroubled by visions or dreams. And then this: stranded on a beach of tangled bed clothes, thoughts wearing ruts in the same cold sand: hesitations and longings, and resentments, many resentments, towards Karel (for being blasé), towards Rose (she had taken advantage, made him feel vulnerable), towards Marietta and towards Godfrey, them most of all in these dark, sleepless hours. Each night, resentments turned over and over until they wore ruts in the sand, until water oozed into them, water stinking of rot and leaving a sourness on the back of his tongue, each resentment actually a guilt and each guilt a doubt, a reason to distrust himself and grow closer to desperation. With desperation came fear. That he would not succeed. Not paint again. Not... That Marietta would have left in any case, that he was the reason for her leaving... That he could not finish the painting, afraid of what finishing might mean, afraid of that fear, afraid of the failure of not completing the canvas, afraid... Afraid that Godfrey would inevitably abandon him... Afraid that... Fearful... Fearing...

Floodtide. Lifted off the beach, out, beyond the breakers into deep water, dead of night dark, hours before dawn.

Sleep unbroken until the alarm clock. Walking out to greet the dawn beyond the walls of the flask. Sleep unbroken by dream or vision.

If there were voices in the darkness, Honza would not know. He did not want to listen. Did not know he should.

Another piece of art had appeared in the studio when he returned next morning: another plaque, of Bacchus this time, carved in ash, the God of Wine wearing the mask of abandon, caught up in the arms of a figure unseen but suggested in the grain and a subtle shaping of the wood. At first glance Bacchus was lost to the world, lost in ecstasy and carnal sensation. Taking another step back, it might be that the god, apparently debased and oblivious, was acting with purpose, but whether that was to find ultimate release by allowing the unseen to draw him into the depths of the void beyond the surface or, instead, draw the unseen out so that it might be anchored here, in this place, this room, Honza could not decide.

'Oh. Where is Godfrey?'

Danvers was taking books from a packing case and laying them out on a side table in the half-moon study.

'Mr Howden has been called away, sir.' Danvers retrieved an envelope from the desk. 'He asked your forgiveness for his absence and that you might read this note.' Danvers stood back, hands clasped as he waited.

Dear Honza,

Forgive my shoving off without a goodbye. Business is a lamentable excuse for interrupting our party. I look forward to resuming our time together. I shall be away a few days at most. In the meantime, I've placed another object in your studio; I believe & trust that the four together will bear fruit.

The house is yours, my dear Honza, and Danvers will act on your word, as ever.

Warmest wishes,

G.

P.S. I'm filled with anticipation at seeing progress on this so vital canvas of yours. Mark my words, it is a masterful work you are bringing into being.

'Is there anything I might do to assist you further, sir?'

Honza looked over the note again. 'I was wondering about the pieces that have been put in the studio, the statues and plaques.'

Danvers raised a polite eyebrow: *Indeed, sir?*

'I'm… finding them distracting. Would you remove them?'

'Mr Howden's gifts, sir?'

'Yes. I don't wish to be ungrateful but I am finding it hard to—'

'I'm afraid Mr Howden's instructions on this matter have been quite explicit, sir.' Danvers's expression was unimpeachably bland.

'In this note…' Honza held up the letter.

'I am to see to your comfort, yes, sir, and I shall endeavour to do that to the utmost in the great majority of cases.'

'But not this case.'

Danvers bowed his head fractionally. 'Mr Howden's instructions were unequivocal.'

She strained against the canvas, wanting to be more than the thickness of a few brushstrokes. With each added detail she turned away from the path she and her companions had followed, towards the circular studio and him. It was there. In the pigment, in her eyes as she looked at him from within the frame of canvas and wood. She was coming closer. Or trying to.

To her right, the smears of paint remained no more substantial than fog, with a fog's reluctance to agree on detail, a fog's desire to remain spectral. If he pushed, sometimes the fog cleared a little. Feather emerged from the body of the figure to Marietta's right, an owl's full moon face crowned by moth's antennæ, the iridescent scales of a great carp forming a cloak across shoulders that twitched and rose into dragonfly gossamer around wolf's torso, hare's forelimbs, the legs of a roe deer, the whole chimera anything but grotesque, anything but fixed no matter how hard he pushed against the fog. But as he pushed—neck and shoulder muscles so tense the pain clamped across his skull, frown of concentration warped into a snarl, physical effort as great as the effort of imagination—as he pushed, so the image shifted again. Another few dabs of paint and gossamer was replaced by feathers, fluoresced into crystal and precious stone as scales became summer sunlight as easily as they might transmute into the midnight sable of a jaguar. The chimera to Marietta's right might be anything, no matter how hard he pushed, but always extraordinary, always taking on forms that spoke of the wondrous in all things. Mutable. Unfixable except that it stayed firmly on the path the three trod together, refusing every effort to give it the solidity that was lifting Marietta out of the canvas and into the round studio.

It was much the same with the companion to her left. Head of sun. Head of moon, waxing at present although, a few days ago, it had been dark, waiting to reveal the first sliver of its reborn face. Of the companion's body, only the pole star heart remained certain and fixed, the rest a shifting landscape of river banks and hillside notches, the belt of Orion around a waist that led to a narrow path between a dense stand of trees that otherwise appeared impenetrable. Beyond, the companion became a track across a broad valley floor, long grass waving under a breeze that rose and fell, warm with the scent of wild thyme and dog rose. Another day and the companion would gather other signs and waymarks into its form, always changing, only heart fixed, and this companion no more willing to climb from the canvas than the other.

Honza stomped across the patio and along the path to the end of the garden, slate flags slippery underfoot, balance precarious in the dull of the afternoon, walls of the flask pressed close, clouds swallowing the mountains and drawing the garden into themselves, the air misty, chill against his skin as he gripped the wooden gate, able to see only a few metres across the hillside before the hillside became mist, unformed, indistinct.

It was impossible.

His legs gave way.

The wall tried to hold him up. Muscles trembled, exhaustion a harrowed line from pit of throat to feathering heart, breath a weight in each lung, chill seeping from the air, from the stone sets beneath arms and pressed against ribs, sodden earth holding up feet, stopping them sliding further, stone and grass the only things holding, stopping this body falling, falling away, thoughts floating—*it was all impossible... all of it... couldn't... couldn't be done... impossible, all*—thoughts would remain if the earth gave way, if rock and stone let go, thoughts would float, random, soured thoughts, heart soured, angered, angry at bone and gut and skull filled with mist and tissue unformed, indistinct, wiped away and painted in again, wiped away and painted, wiped away and if pushed, pushed so that concentration became a snarl and breath a scream, if pushed—*it's impossible, all of it*—if pushed then there was only mist, unfixed, only dim light, unformed. Only thoughts, floating. Only the pain of muscles exhausted, bones weary to the point of breaking, fingers cramped, eyes blurred, misted and formless. Only a heart, beating. Each beat a sorrow, a failure. Each sorrow a prick of gooseflesh, a twitch of muscle. That joint. This eye. Another tear falling. As the body would. Fall...

'Sir? Might I suggest you shelter under this umbrella? And, also, take advantage of this blanket, sir? If you will forgive me, I have taken the liberty of laying a fire in the sitting room grate and have water ready to brew hot tea. There is also, sir, water warming for a bath. If you will allow me to suggest that you should partake of each of these comforts, sir...?'

It was hard to move. The body—Honza's body—had grown cold and numb. He managed to nod, the effort of standing almost too much, so that he swayed as Danvers wrapped the blanket across his shoulders, angling the umbrella to shelter Honza from the rain coalescing out of the mist.

'Have...' Throat (his throat) quite dry. 'Have I been out here long?'

It was well after sundown.

'I fear so, sir.' Danvers took his elbow firmly, supporting each step as they turned to the house, urging Honza to stay by the fire. 'I have a change of clothes at present in the airing cupboard, warming. If you are able to wait just a few moments, sir...?'

Honza let him fuss, following each instruction, too lost in the novelty of rediscovering a sense of himself and of his body.

Flames shimmied, gyred, their heat making his face and hands smart, throb, skin feel tight. He did not move away from the fire.

The deep chill from the rain and the darkening hillside had passed into other sensations that on another occasion might have been accepted without notice. This night, he sat beside the hearth in his bedroom, feeding the fire a little wood now and then, and explored each one: the aftertaste of herbs from the infusion Danvers had brought a short while ago; the feeling in his gut as dinner slowly digested; a heaviness in the legs and back from a long time soaking in the bath... Each a novelty as if he had never experienced anything of the sort before.

Danvers had wanted to place hot water bottles in the bed, bank the fire in the hearth, tidy the bedroom to make it more comfortable for sir. Honza had politely declined and, when that had not worked, asked Danvers to leave him alone. A ragged thread in his mind had set light with each new intrusion. It urged him to shout and rage at Danvers, an instinctive turn towards anger and hostility. Yet, in those same moments, Honza had found himself watching Danvers hover, Danvers make another offer to organise loose sketches, drawing materials, the portfolio, left out and open, uppermost sketch turned face down across it, inviting anxiety from Honza and clearly encouraging curiosity in Danvers. Firm in declining all offers, Honza had been aware of the rush of pulse and adrenaline, tension wanting to hunch his shoulders, curl his fingers, tightness bringing acid to the pit of his throat. Aware of each bodily change he had felt distant and unmoved by them, conscious that aggression was a choice not a necessity.

'I'll call if I want anything but I'm very tired, I'm sure I shall be asleep soon. Thank you for all your help and attention.'

No anger, not even sarcasm, in his voice and Danvers, face neutral, with no choice but to leave the room.

Another piece of wood on the fire. Heat a scalpel flensing aside skin in search of bone. Flamelight reaching to point to a detail, or indicate a whole sketch, encouraging the sepia pencil lines to fade into the paper and leave only the essence of each drawing behind. An island, the sea, a cottage, a path. A figure...

His body and these drawings were part of the same thing.

The intuition returned and Honza had to admit he did not understand what it meant, scepticism dropping away, such thoughts nothing more than excuses not to listen. Honza picked up a drawing—shallow bay, sweep of sand beneath shaggy grass, land rising, nestling the ruins of a church in its billow and swell, church a suggestion in the pencil strokes because it was not visible from this vantage (he knew this without question) and yet still it was there.

No memory of the act of drawing, not this sketch any more than the others. Yet still the intuition remained, anything else an excuse not to listen, the answer to every

doubt already there for him, answered by Elnara weeks ago.
Listen to your heart.

Four clay lamps burned in the round studio, dishes possibly as old as they appeared, wicks floating in scented oils. Kronos, Pan, Bacchus, Helios as king of them all placed due North, each on a cardinal point, a fact noticed and driven from mind by the frustration of completing Marietta's picture. And the oil lamps intercardinal between each god.

Two standard lamps positioned either side of the easel, Honza blew out the flames and settled in front of the canvas: Marietta's face; the ghost forms of her companions, sketched in and rubbed out. The canvas looked back, their gazes meeting half way.

Taking up a brush and pausing and letting it rest in an open palm. Watching.

Waiting. Listening
listening
listening

silence

silence

which contained an answer. In a line of paint. Or sepia pencil.

Do you know what this means?
Do you know what you have done?

New day tapping at the windows.

Night yawned and took another step westwards, dawn clambering up the hills, new day slipping between shadows and fading rain to the window, to peer around the glow of standard lamps angled to expel shadow, Helios eyes-closed and Bacchus distracted, wineskin forgotten, new day tapping at the window. Beckoning.

Flagpath slick and slippery, rain fading to needle-pricks on air cool and still stained at the edges with indigo, shadows clotted against the foot of the stone wall, not moving to help when balance proved too uncertain to climb up onto the top, a whole night of sitting between electric lights, before canvas, brush and paint close to hand, leaving muscles stiff and joints creaking, grass soft underfoot, willing to support another attempt to scramble to the top of the wall. Air a cold tonic, eyes relaxing with the turn eastwards.

Hills in silhouette beginning to fill out and acquire mass, form becoming apparent as the rain drew back, new day pushing cloud aside and presenting the first gleam of sun, sunlight burnishing the hillside, gilding a hand raised, fingers spread to touch light that transmuted raindrops and spider's webs into diamond and opal. New day chill, cool welcome. Muscles loosening and arms spread as this dawn pushed back the clouds and opened the flask.

A motorcar wound closer along the lane towards the front of the house, engine's voice cleaving the air, gravel rasping and a door slamming in answer. Circling a second time, a crow barked, word lost on the breeze and the sound of more doors slamming inside the house, voices raised.

He looked away from the sunrise, afterimages crawling over the house. Lights were visible in the round studio. A cry carried along the garden.

Honza turned back to the sunrise, eastern sky running clear and cloudless.

Another door slammed, voice barging about.

The crow turned westward, following the rain out across the Irish Sea.

The backdoor opened, leather heels hacked against slate flags. Honza looked across the valley, a last glance before climbing off the wall as Godfrey strode down the garden.

Afterwards began with the lanes taking him down through the hills towards the village, to hesitate at a road sign, unwilling to decide which fork to take and leaving Honza to choose for himself, incline growing steeper beneath him, oaks of beaten copper too tired by the growing lateness of the year to walk all the way to the top of the hill with him, hilltop left open to diamond-cut sunshine and circling rooks, calling gulls inscribing the blue.

This was how afterwards began.

No suitcase. No overcoat. Only the clothes he had on. This light, this unburdened, it was easy to wander, to veer away from the coast, down lanes, hedgerows parting to present a field ploughed and furrowed, a field planted with winter crop or mobbed by rooks that gave him not even a second glance, engine droning in the distance, fretting over a gear change, rattling over potholes, drone coming closer until the small delivery van trundled past at little more than a brisk walking pace to pull into the verge.

'Need a lift, mate? Going far?'

Honza was going to say he was happy to walk and instead asked, 'Do know a well? And a ruined cottage?'

The van driver wondered if he meant Ffynnon Gybi and told Honza to hop in. Before there was chance to remember if this was the name Godfrey Howden had told him, the van lurched as the driver wrestled it into third gear.

The smell of fresh bread filled the cab.

'Hungry? Help yourself.' And one hand in the vicinity of the steering wheel, the driver tugged aside the window between the cab and the back of the van.

Honza's stomach rumbled.

'Won't your employer…?'

'Work for myself, see.' The driver waved towards the trays framed by the window.

'I can pay.' His stomach rumbled and grew tight with thoughts of eating: how long since his last meal, long before he might eat again.

'You look all in. This one's on me. Go on—' The driver waved towards the bread, van slewing, making a wave of invitation of its own.

He had a delivery to make first, if that was alright? Honza munched slowly, chewing on a piece of crust: the baker was welcome to do whatever was on his itinerary.

'You're foreign?' Sunlight fell through the windscreen, the baker's hands broad and pink on the wheel, van pulling away from a corner shop, hamlet hidden by a bend in the road.

'I'm Czech, Bohemian. From Prague.'

'My wife was foreign, see, English.' The baker watched the road, giving Honza only a profile to study. 'She died, three years ago next January.'

'My condolences. I lost someone recently. Not dead but gone.'

'Still hurts though, eh?' Silence of engine and road and the soft whisper of bread being torn. The baker sighed. 'I still speak to her. Try to, you know.' The van slowed as the baker search for the right turning. 'Spiritualist Church, see,' the baker explained. 'Do you believe?'

'I… don't know, anymore.'

The van slowed to a pause.

'My wife was a Theosophist, read all them books, Madame Blavatsky and Mr Steiner and Mr Krishnamurti and Mrs Bessant and others, lots of books. She believed she would come back, reincarnate. Eventually.' The baker peered through the windscreen.

Endless blue.

'I can't wait, see. Not that long.' The driver opened his door. 'Have to walk from here.'

Broken walls rose from the dense grass and waited.

A breeze smoothed over the surface of the well. Honza knelt beside the water, the baker stiffly settling on the opposite side of the cistern. Sunlight brought out the scent of grass and lichen-covered rock. Old leaves settled closer to the earth, each a moment, a thought. Summer's passing and long nights dreaming ahead tinged each breath, autumn's perfume.

A raven settled on the wall. A raven spoke, black wingtip, obsidian eye. Honza nodded and they looked into the well, faces light and shadow, shadow and light spread across the face of the well, depths beneath masked if not entirely hidden.

'Everyone—' The baker cleared his throat. 'Everyone has a guardian angel.'

Faces on the surface, the trees rooted, raven on the wing. Endless blue.

'A word like "demon", see? Greek.'

'Yes.'

'Everyone. I…'

But the baker kept silent, as did the well. A breeze ruffled the grass, heading westward. Honza looked away from the well. A voice spoke. A voice had spoken, not his own. Tears prickled, hollowing throat and chest. Hunching, swallowing a breath, pain not fading, the breeze pointing westward and the faces motionless across the surface of the well, water blue, endless blue.

'Your loss.' The baker hardly whispered. 'The person gone…'

Honza could not move.

'How?'

Breath copper, hitched in throat. (*Do you know what this means? Do you know what you've done?*) Voice the raven's when he swallowed, managed: 'I sent her away.'

'You bloody fool.'

Godfrey Howden wiped spittle from his mouth.

'You've no idea, do you?'

Honza sat on the stone wall, not calm, anxiety a clamour trembling hands and knees, urging he should run, he should shout back, words there in mind and in the tight muscles of shoulders and throat.

Honza sat, sunshine warm against his face in spite of the edge to the easterly pushing the last of the cloud away.

Flask broken apart.

'Oh, of course.' Howden looked as though he had not slept, certainly in a day, perhaps in days, skin glistening and flushed, mouth no longer so louche. 'The contemptible Greer.'

'I haven't spoken to Rose since—'

'Indeed. But you know, you damn well—'

'I'm not sure what—'

'*Danvers!*' Howden spun and bellowed down the length of the garden. Honza managed to stand without weaving, aware of the distance between him and Godfrey Howden, only a few steps. Of how easy it would be to clamber over the wall and retreat down the hillside.

'I'm grateful for your hospitality.' He took a step towards Howden.

'The hell you are.' Howden yelled down the garden again.

'But—'

'Sit down.'

'No.'

'You bastard, I'll—'

Back door flung open, Danvers almost tripping over the step, canvas unwieldy in his hands as he skidded on damp flagstones, scuttling towards them. Paint smeared his hands, Honza noted, the painting finished but yet to dry.

'This won't stop me.' Howden ordered Danvers to hold the picture steady, damn it. 'No matter what you think.'

'She will not come,' Honza replied, not entirely sure what he meant.

'Damn you, you bastard,' Howden snarled, taking a step back from the painting, the sight of it repellant.

Marietta. Her two companions. Her face turned away from the viewer, figure altered so that instead of striding forwards, out of the picture frame, the painting captured her on the point of veering away, face decisive where earlier the pigment had suggested uncertainty, hesitation. A sun now found itself on the cusp of the treeline, sunrise fixing a cardinal point and that point orienting her turn. Southwards. Wherever she was, she was now heading south with her companions. And her companions—

'Why Marietta?' The tremor in his voice was hardly noticeable. 'Why her?'

'Damn the woman, why should I ever care—' Howden snatched the canvas from Danvers, the servant almost falling with the violence of the action.

'Her companions, the Compass and the Notebook—' Godfrey Howden brandished the painting.

Honza flinched, sure Howden was going to strike him.

'Her companions...' Howden shook the painting, its stretcher creaking as his shoulders trembled.

On one side of Marietta there had been owl-faced moth, wolf-dragonfly, a moment sublime; on the other, pole star and moon and landscape guiding a path whose end was still too far away to know with certainty. Both gone, obliterated by brushstroke and pigment. Instead, the companions were fixed in shape, form, their faces and expressions simply the random work of imagination and whim. Or so it had seemed at first, until late towards dawn he had felt certain there was nothing random in the faces Marietta's companions had adopted: a man, deep-tanned by unwavering sunlight, hair a dandelion clock that marked time and impulse more completely than the sweep of a shadow under the sun or the tide's marriage to the moon; and a woman, younger, taller, pale as alabaster and pure as winter ice, her eyes sunsets offering dreams and a tomorrow as perfect as today.

These were Marietta's companions.

'They will not come,' Honza told Howden.

The flush left Godfrey Howden's face. He stood, straight and calm, voice quite as emotionless as Honza's. 'Get out of my house.'

'My clothes—'

'Get out, Mr Pernath. Now.'

Godfrey Howden put his fist through the canvas.

A raven's wing against the sun, shadow travelling over the van.

Neither of them moved.

'And the voice told you…?'

'Perhaps it was instinct.'

Blue tempered. And shadows longer. Sun drawn towards the horizon, drawn westward.

'But, see, you heard it as a voice, didn't you?'

Afterwards had begun with a word: *Walk*. And he had said nothing but climbed the wall and walked through the new-day sunshine, down-slope to the lanes. That was how afterwards had begun. Not with Howden, clinical in his fury as he destroyed the painting. Afterwards had begun with a voice and word.

'But you heard a voice,' the baker had said as they returned to the van. A little later, as a raven wing crossed the sun, Honza murmured, 'Perhaps it was instinct.'

'But still.'

Honza nodded.

Blue, sky still blue and no cloud, damp coming down, cool to the touch, sharp on the nostrils. Touched with brine.

'I'll drive you.' The baker thumbed the starter. 'I know a cove, a man with a boat.'

The drawings, sepia: low-skipping shoreline, slope of hill rising into a mountain, a house and a ruined church. The baker had known the island as soon as Honza begun describing it. Island of bards and saints. A lighthouse; ruined church part of an ancient abbey. The house might be one of several but the shore remained unmistakable.

'It's late. We've been here hours—someone must be expecting you, your shop, customers.'

'No one, not really.' The baker took off the handbrake. 'Besides, you're not the only one, are you? To hear voices, your angel's voice, eh?'

'In the morning,' the boatman said. And so it was.

Honza did not dream that night, sleeping on coiled ropes in the chandlery, moon drawing waves from the cove, westward.

The island waited.

The boatman dropped him off in the shallows, a short way from the beach.

Sunlight rode each wavecrest, sky empty of anything other than sun and circling birds.

Honza waved, waiting until the boat was beyond the breakwater heading back to the mainland, eastwards.

The bay was much as he had drawn it, shallow beach rising gradually into low hillsides, mountain forming a crest to the north. Buildings hunkered into the contours of the land, none especially familiar, none the house he was looking for. To the south, the bay curved away, forming a low headland on which a lighthouse rose, tower foursquare towards the oncoming waves, the single light, a cyclops eye, able to sweep across the whole island.

Gulls circled, swooping across the ribbon of beach to bank, soar over the breakwater and into endless blue beyond, day warm against Honza's face, breeze from the sea whispering, humming, searching for a scrap of tune or a thought half-forgotten, each syllable brine-touched, like the waves that crackled, hissed syllables of their own. Perhaps.

Honza followed a rough track leading inland, wishing things were different, although he was unsure how they should be. Perhaps that he was less afraid. Perhaps that.

Few people lived on the island. Famers, some. A painter, watercolour on an easel and easel pointing out to sea. They talked for a while. She had never seen the house Honza described, never seen the man he believed lived there. No, he told her when she asked if he had the wrong island. The painter offered him food, tea, but Honza was not hungry, although he had not eaten since the day before. Water was all he wanted.

Only a few hours to walk the whole island round. She pointed out the path to the ruined abbey: he was welcome to come by on his return.

Part of an old chapel, a graveyard behind iron railings nearby. And older ruins, the abbey waiting just along the lane. A farmer trudged past pushing a cart filled with hay. He had no recollection of the house either. Together they trundled the cart along the lane, unloaded it, sheep bleating, one nudging Honza. A thank you.

Black outcrops of rock hunkered to peer down at the waves, horizon a lens bending sky into sea, water into air. Honza clambered over one of the outcrops to look for himself

Rattle of metal, tyres rasping as a bell trilled.

The cyclist waved a greeting, curve of the hillside stepping between them before Honza had chance to react. Hill rising, climbing over itself, a series of breasts and knolls as the low mountain gathered to cut an outline against the blue overhead. Honza waited. No one stepped over the crest of the lowest knoll, no one stood in silhouette higher up.

A narrow inlet cut a thin wedge from the cliffside, swells lifting and falling away from the bare rock walls. A face appeared between the waves, whiskers white, eyes liquid, deepest night.

Soundless, without trace, the seal dipped back beneath the surface.

The water appeared black, shadows from the walls of the inlet, the black rocks, water polished obsidian. No sign of his own reflection, the distance too great.

Honza waited in case the seal reappeared. A detachment had held him since climbing over the garden wall, since meeting the baker. It faded a little, wind plucking at his jacket, bringing a shiver in spite of the sun. Thoughts and imaginings plucking much as the breeze plucked. Seeing the painting finished as Godfrey Howden had expected, Marietta walking up to the house in response to its summons. He found himself restaging yesterday morning here, amidst black rocks and waves, Honza fearless, Honza snatching the canvas from Danvers, Honza—

What does your heart say?

Elnara might have been standing behind him, voice clear and close. Her voice. A voice.

He gazed over the rocks, inland. No one. Not on the road, the low rise behind.

Honza told himself it had been a bird passing, or wishful thinking, this wanting to see someone on the rise, watching.

There was no answer when he returned to the painter's house. It was past midday, lengthening shadows drawing the sun lower, sea breeze cooler, the stones of the ruined abbey chill beneath him as he sat, watching the lane, expecting the farmer to return, sometime.

No one came by.

Honza glanced towards the nearest crest of hillside.

No one stood on it.

Another walk around the island brought no more sign of the cottage in the sketches than had the first. The path lay back from the sea, higher than the waves as it swung towards the shallow bay. The lighthouse cast a sundial's shadow, back turned towards the mainland to watch his approach, mainland nothing more than a drift of smoke clinging to the horizon.

Only him and the lighthouse.

A razorbill made a sweep, carving another circle through the air, another after that, another…

Him, the lighthouse and the birds, the seals bridging air and water, water and land. No one crossed between the buildings at the foot of the lighthouse. No one stood in their gardens or walked the road around the island. Only Honza.

Dusk crept closer, advancing between the waves.

Shadows lengthened. And the mountain, dark against the sun, dissolved into motes, afterimages wandering along the track to the bay, changing colour, form.

Shade of his hand falling across his eyes, Honza squinted, gaze flitting, back, there, back, only to dismiss the idea that he had seen anyone at all. He settled amongst the rough grass and faced the sea. After a time a voice stuttered. *Ch-ch… ch-ch…* Wings stroking air into earth. Red beak, black feathers gleaming, red claws.

Red and black.

A red-billed crow.

The bird stood. Motionless.

Only the grass moved, the breeze and the creep of dusk.

At last, the bird in red and black tilted its head, gazing along the track towards the cottages, the mountain masking the sun's face.

Honza was unsure. And when the lighthouse roused, eye sweeping across island, across waves, across Honza, foghorn sounding, once, even though the late afternoon was clear and the very first stars glinted, he startled, shivering as he stood and peered, colour draining from the day, thread of track little more than a pale line. No lights showing in any of the cottages. No sign anyone had been watching.

The lighthouse went dark after nightfall, leaving the stars to hang in whatever position they had been holding when the light went out. Waves hissed, susurration breathing in with each swell, out on the ebb, waves tugging, Honza little more than flotsam. He lay amongst the marram grass above the shore, staring at the night staring down at him, mind empty but for the waves, the press of hard earth against bone and flesh, blades of grass cradling his head, the complaints of joints unmoved in the last hours or centuries, cold a presence, part of skin and muscle as he was a part of the cold, night unflinching as he cried, thoughts of Marietta repeating, thoughts of Marietta repeating the same moments, finding her note, garret becoming round studio, Bacchus and Pan, Helios turned to the wall, note tucked beneath it, the note torn up, flung in the face of Godfrey Howden, or Rose Greer, the note tucked beneath a water glass… a tube of paint… the note…

The night watched and made no comment and hunger remembered itself to him and the form and presence of himself, in this muscle, that sinew, in blink and breath and smell of brine and grass, became all there was, until it was hard to know where the shore ended and this form and presence, this Honza, began, and Honza opened his eyes, sure he had been dreaming, sitting up to watch the black sun gather the night about itself, which surely meant he was asleep after all.

He woke to a vision of Marietta standing on the other side of the bay, unable to come closer, her voice indistinct although her disappointment was clear, her distress that he had altered the painting instead of—

Tears ran down his face.

A fog swathed the island, altering distance, erasing sea and sun. Its dank essence sank into his bones, each movement stiff and palsied as he levered himself out of the marram, hunger wearing his outerself, an ill-fitting suit, its weakness gnawing at his spirit.

Marietta's voice came out of the mist.

No sign of her, no matter how long he waited, dew against his face, dew trickling down his cheeks.

The first cottage he came to was locked, no lights, no answer. Honza stared along the narrow lane, trying to remember the sketches. The house had been here, sometimes.

Fool.

Godfrey Howden leaned against the drystone wall dividing the patch of garden from the field next door.

Honza ignored him.

A few of the cottages were unlocked. All unoccupied. Howden waited for Honza to finish his search of each before telling him again he was a fool.

All you had to do was finish the picture, Godfrey drawled as they followed the narrow road around the island, mist hiding the mountaintop, hiding the ruins until Honza thought they must be gone, like the house in the sketches or the figure watching in the distance.

He was going to ignore Howden. Howden was, anyway, an hallucination.

It wouldn't have been right, he told Howden.

One person's right is another person's wrong.

The mist swirled aside to present Rose Greer waiting beside the ruins of the ancient abbey.

There is no right and wrong, only the will to act, Rose told him as he reached for the crumbling stones.

You used me, hurt me, he told her, unable to find what he searched for.

I only did what you do, with brushes and paint—

And pencils and paper.

Godfrey Howden held up one of the sketches of the island. Honza tried to snatch it back. The mist took it, erasing the last pencil line before making the paper fade away.

A gull cried out and its voice was Marietta's.

Honza strode down the road, determined not to run, foot catching a pothole, stumble making him feel foolish although there was no one to see it.

You are a fool, Godfrey Howden reminded him.

Honza yelled at the mist to shut up.

But the mist ate away the mountaintop and the sky. It erased the sea, leaving only the hiss of surf, only shingle and sand in the bay, the rocks at the entrance merging into the mist, mist turning about itself, ignoring Honza.

He yelled louder.

The fog horn answered, voice deadened by the haze until it was hardly anything at all. Only a murmur.

Foolish.

Godfrey Howden smiled and produced sketchbook, charcoal, a sketch of Honza in dunce's cap and motley, broken paintbrush in hand.

At least she didn't die, the baker told him.

Shut up. Honza spat at the mist. Shut up and leave me, leave me—

Rose Greer tugged at his sleeve. He will not come, you know.

She shook her head and the motion was a breeze through the grass.

Shut up, Honza pleaded.

At least she didn't die, the baker reminded him.

As good as dead, Godfrey Howden reminded him.

Drove her away, Rose Greer reminded him.

Will there be anything more, sir? Danvers asked, tearing up the last of the sepia sketches.

Sand and shingle, slithering, weaving, line of footprints behind, nothing in front until he found the waves, retreating tide hidden in the mist. They spoke and it sounded like Marietta. The lighthouse added its voice. Honza told it to stay out of it. Honza told the waves it was all wrong. It's all wrong, the baker agreed, it's not like in the books. It's all like the books, Rose Greer declared as she waded out into the water. We must write the books, Godfrey Howden contended, sea already level with his chest.

Honza thrashed at the waves, thrashed at the air and the mist, voice coming back to him in gulps and sobs and the hollow mourning of the foghorn and the breeze turning westward, saltwater tears and saltwater thoughts and the spasm of another bout of rage, or sorrow, another attempt at holding on to what was lost.

Lost.

All of it lost.

The rage and the anguish would not leave him, even as the mist cleared, as the waves turned back towards the island and urged him to retreat beyond the tideline to the long grass at the edge of the bay. A point came when it seemed there was no more, not tears nor the energy for rage. With it, fresh tears. Tears unshed since Hampstead, tears unshed since Prague. And it began to feel, with each new outpouring, that it was the sea that was streaming from his eyes, that he was the sea, an inlet in the bay, another headland on which a lighthouse could stand and see in all directions. And when the grief became shallow, when the pain of doubt and second-guessing grew colder, so the sea climbed over sand and shingle, foam glimmering in the darkness as it reached for him, cursing, reciting lamentations, half-remembered liturgies, spitting through those parts where memory failed and the pain of being, the sheer physical ache of wavecrest and sinew and cold night air and the prospect of living through all this again another day, rose against the ragged edges of the island and channeled through him, to burst into hoarse shouts and pleadings, recriminations and threats, a dozen entreaties emptying into another swell, another foaming wave.

The lighthouse grew dark.
Constellations tilted, hung in silence, each star a pinprick, the night not infinite after all, not if it could be pricked, if a dim light shone from somewhere behind it.
A little owl shrilled.
Sprawled in the long grass. Two goes to sit up, muscles spent, no strength to walk. Lighthouse a pale shape, bay more sound than form. Gaps between the stars that might have been clouds, might have been voids.
Night.
The owl called again.
Rubbing the skin around each eye, tears dry but vision uncertain still.

The star remained. Fixed, directly ahead, just above where the sea might end and the sky begin.

Sunlight brushed against his face.
 A breeze swayed the grass. The sun touched him again. Forehead, eyes, lingering on a cheek. Encouraging him to wake, slowly sit up. Joints popped, muscles gathering a host of complaints, pains fleet or lingering, all recounting something of yesterday, not gone but past.
 The sun was high: late morning, towards noon. Light warm against his face, outstretched hands. Honza remembered the bread the widower baker had given him, each crumb, each morsel, memory bringing saliva and an ache in his stomach. He tried to count how long ago that loaf of bread must be; two days seemed too short a time.
 Honza let the sun warm him.
 A few clouds, birds, a breeze that rode on the waves and whispered.
 Honza half-listened. Aware of pressure in his bladder, the need to find fresh water. Letting each thought pass. Gazing across the bay. Star faint but visible if he turned his head and looked sidelong, the moon a ghost over the curve of the mountain.

The crow with red beak and red feet was waiting for him when he came out of the painter's cottage. The door had been locked, the key on a hook beside the door. A wash, bladder relieved. There was food but he left it untouched, wanting to keep fasting and not questioning the impulse.
 The crow blinked.

Red and black, sun pale as winter and autumn damp filling each breath, each shadow.
 Birds wheeled, keeping their distance.

Honza sat among the black rocks, watching for seals as he turned over thoughts, memories, unsure whether he expected to find anything. Of Rose and Godfrey, no sign; the baker, likewise, absent.

It was catharsis.

It was epiphany.

It was…

Honza let the thought trail away and watched the sea, swells foaming against the walls of the inlet. Now and then he glanced up, searching for sign of the star, the moon, both hidden by the mountain or the sun's westward track. He turned to the waves, black, and white foam against the rocks. He never thought to look to the horizon, see if anyone was watching.

Stones lay in two piles, a few loaded into a wheelbarrow. A drystone wall in the making, a sheepfold. Something unrealised.

Honza trundled the barrow down to the bay, casting about until he found a spot along the curve of the shore leading towards the lighthouse, tamping down the grass to make a place to begin work.

After the first few courses it was easy to see it was not going right. Taking away the stones, Honza dropped his jacket into the grass, rolled up his sleeves and began again, laying the first stones in a circle as a foundation for the whole.

The crow with red beak and red feet settled on the edge of the wheelbarrow. It made no comment and the dusk gathered about them with as much noise, only the sound of rock against rock.

Honza stood back. The sun, hunkered low over the sea, extended his shadow until it brushed against the foot of the cairn. It was going to be bigger than he had first envisaged. Honza wiped sweat from his forehead, tugging on his jacket as he climbed the gentle rise towards the lighthouse.

A beacon fire on top, he thought, looking back. The lighthouse sounded a single, low note, tone rolling out over the waves towards the night, lighthouse making a belfry of the sky in which to hang the evening star. Honza stretched out his hand but it was the wrong star and when the incoming tide answered the lighthouse's call it reminded him to be patient.

The lighthouse sounded another long, low note.

First light.

Honza took the barrow back to the piles of stones and loaded enough rock to keep him going until the sun rose.

The cairn grew taller.

Sunrise: russet gold, shadows where there had been grey, waves hissing, another stone fitted into place, stone cold, stone like the air, breath hanging over stone cold, hands casting shadows, breeze a passing birdwing, gullwing, gannet a shadow, pink shading into red-orange, russet-gold wind clouds earth-damp smell mud still-damp under rock rocks fetched rocks piled next rock fitted cool hand-rock-sunrise shadow-call bird-wave-hiss sunrising mist-into-sky smell of russet-gold water-into-air sound of sun against face-hands rock burnished earth-into-fire into feel of the click rock against rock into breath into pile into fit into movement into hiss and foam and shadows growing small growing into sun and new day and rock fitted into place.

And so the cairn grew taller.

The cairn was finished by afternoon.

Wood scavenged and stacked in the hollow cup of its top.

Grass rustling, wind picking at the small pile of branches and driftwood set aside to feed the flames later.

After sunset.

Waking. Sun resting on the other side of the island. Grown cold while asleep. Walking stiffly along the spur of headland towards the lighthouse, muscles aching. Hunger accepted, both part of the earth underfoot. An oystercatcher circled. Lifting a hand towards the sun. Turning east and reaching for the coming night still hidden in the distance. Waiting, first star gradually opening its eye. Less aware of hand-arm-shoulder than hand-air-sea-dusk, which was part of spindrift-foam-beach-grass, of land-sea, of…

Watching the night approach over the waves, all thought slipped away.

First twigs catching. Another match, the reek of sulphur clawing at brine and night air. More kindling. Flames chattering, eager. Adding more twigs, firelight waving, turning about itself. A piece of branch. Next after that bringing the call of an owl, a scent of woodsmoke musky and resinous against the breeze and the sea's breath.

Beacon fire.

Sparks rose through the darkness, wanting to greet the stars, join the stars, losing their way and tumbling, firelight strong enough to reach through the night into blackness, hiding sea and much of the island beyond this pool of light.

More branches. More flames. Beaconlight an island to itself, this place and nothing more, nothing beyond the glow of fire. Hands held out to the sparks floating, motes bronze, molten gold, winking out. More following, always rising, falling, rising. Heat part of flesh, sinking, into sinew, into bone, fire teasing ghostshapes out of the dark, each one a part of the fire, part of this island of light which watched the tumbling sparks and put more wood on the fire and wiped at a nose running from the heat and laughed and gasped at the sound and laughed again and felt tears dry in the heat and laughed again and drew breath and felt a pulse beating in sympathy with the flames and with the hiss and whisper of the waves somewhere nearby, nearby as a hand wiped away the last dried tear.

Last of the wood.

Flames dwindling, falling into embers, embers coming alive with a breath, with a breath of wind.

As the fire lessened so the blackness lessened. Stars, not sparks after all, and the lighthouse a white shape not quite solid in the near-distance. New moon a sliver, high overhead. One bright star, low, to the east.

Embers into ash. Fire still warm against a palm.

Clambering through the long, stiff grass, up the shallow incline until the ground grew more level, night drawing aside to reveal the black sun hanging between the stars, its glow defining each contour and every shadow.

'You should wake up now and drink this.'

The old man was hunkered in the grass beside him. Steam rose from a metal cup. Fire popped, the smell of smoke reminiscent of the cairn, the beacon light.

'Broth.' The man held out the metal cup, holding it by the lip. 'It's hot.'

'Oh.'

Honza managed to sit, perfume of woodsmoke and ash rising from his clothes, soot on his hands as he took the cup, managing nothing more than inhaling steam on the first attempt, stomach suddenly tight, throat clamping at the taste of saliva.

'Sip as it cools.' The old man dipped another mug into the pot resting over the campfire.

Sunrise.

Honza could not stop shivering, jaw clamped against the tremors, wincing as he cradled the metal cup, heat welcome so he held it closer still.

High overhead, pinned to the zenith, the black sun neither blinked nor wavered. A thin fret gauzed the sea, ash grey where the sun had yet to touch it. It looked like smoke. The cairn stood partially in silhouette, in shadow. Wings black, beak and feet red. The bird watched them break fast.

'Brân goesgoch.'

The old man nodded a greeting and the bird nodded back.

'It means red-legged crow.'

Honza sipped—herbs, mild, and vegetables: carrots, parsnip—sipped and resisted an urge to gulp. His stomach griped and relaxed again.

'I thought I was seeing things.'

'You were but that doesn't make what you saw unreal.' The old man offered the red-legged crow a salute. 'As real as that one.'

The bird made no reply.

'Have we met? Your voice…' Honza studied the man: hair white and silver, cut close, cut uneven so the man must be trimming his hair himself, high forehead, brow tanned by the weather, lined by time and experience, white stubble, cheeks fleshy but hollowed, little else going spare on his frame, an old and patched gabardine mackintosh clinched tight, a frayed tartan muffler, hands raw, tanned, liver-spotted and oddly delicate. Gaze travelling back over his face, lines around his eyes, eyes—

Honza looked away, self-conscious. 'I'm sorry…'

'You've been searching.'

Honza sipped broth, cup easier to hold as it cooled.

'I don't know.' The cup was empty. The old man took it, along with his own, down to the shore's edge, rinsing them in the waves, hefting the soup pot to one side and smothering the campfire with sand.

'What do you remember?'

'I don't know.' Honza frowned. 'Everything, I think.'

'That's a good place to start.'

The old man took him to a cottage on the north side of

the island, near the abbey ruins. Honza stared at the cottage, a flash of recognition jibing against a conviction he had never seen the house before. A single room downstairs, walls whitewashed. A small table, two chairs, a wooden pallet in the corner opposite the hearth.

'Sleep.'

'But—'

'No, no, you need rest. I'll wake you later, so you can eat.' The old man guided him to the pallet, mattress surprisingly comfortable, wool blanket smelling of camomile.

Honza slept.

It was evening when the old man woke him. More broth, hunk of bread floating in the bowl.

A fire burned in the hearth.

'We can talk tomorrow,' the old man said when Honza tried to eat and speak. Honza content to nod, not sure what he had been about to say. Content to nod.

To sleep.

Waking, leaving the cottage.

Sleep. Pallet creaking softly with each movement. Breathing. Sound of surf. Of the wind. Sleep becoming waking.

Waking, leaving the cottage.

Waking, leaving.

Waking

and stretching, Honza sat up, room cool and sibilant with wave lap, tide rolling, rolling back.

From the door it was short walk to the bay, a handful of metres.

Deep breath: brine, cool air damp on the tongue and prickling his skin, light sea fret glazing the tide and smudging the outline of the lighthouse. Poised overhead, the black sun engraved a white edge around each weak shadow.

The top of the cairn was blackened with soot, the reek of ash grown faint.

'She knew what she wanted, didn't she?'

Voice close to his ear.

Honza glanced at the cairn and turned towards the cottage, the lighthouse. The waves moved, seeing no need to pause. Only go on.

'Marietta, I mean.'

Voice familiar.

He closed his eyes. 'Yes, she was… I don't know. Dedicated?'

'That's not how it felt.'

Honza kept silent but opened his eyes and turned to the cairn.

No cairn. The stones dismantled into piles, a broad disk taking shape on the rough grass, stones remaining to add to complete the circle.

'I didn't understand.'

'But do you now?'

'You—'

The cairn stood again, disk yet to come into being although some of the stones had been removed, piles growing, red-legged crow standing on the remains of the mound.

'You know the answer to that.' Honza wiped mist from his face, suddenly hot despite the breeze off the waves.

'I might not,' the voice murmured close to his ear, 'and

the secret is for you to know.'

'What secret?'

The crow spread its wings. Red and black. Black and red. It did not take off, not quite gone from the earth, not yet wholly of the air.

'An open secret,' the voice replied. 'A secret in name. Because no one listens. Only rarely.'

The sun—the sun of the day, the sun that turned with the earth, each hand in hand—the sun was long past its zenith, shadows thrown eastward. Over the lighthouse the black sun hung, unmoving, a circle of jet, bottomless, endless, unfathomable.

'Just listen,' the voice advised.

Honza began to reply. And remained silent, unsure what this silence meant, watching the waves, watching until it might have been the voice he heard, or no voice at all.

With a flap, the red-legged crow left the cairn, black and red, soot and ash staining the top few courses of stone, staining his hands as Honza began to dismantle what he had built, transmuting stone pile into something

across the short swathe of heath towards the bay. The lighthouse turned, surveying a sea restive, an island poised under the stars, owl invisible as it moved through the darkness, the sound of its wings the wind's breath, or Honza's own.

He stood in the cottage doorway, lighthouse beam passing overhead. With each return of darkness, the stars grew brighter, black sun distinguished by the absence of stars, nothing more, night and black sun one and the same as the beam swung again to spill across the cottage, over the heath and down towards the bay.

A glimmer. That was all the disk was from here beneath the lighthouse, grass and lay of the land hiding most of the stones, memory having to fill in, see arcs of rock, circumference whole and finished, only the very centre to complete.

'Will it be tomorrow?' Honza asked as the old man came to the doorway, peering up at the lighthouse tower above them.

'Only you know that.' The old man walked out into the waiting night, beam finding him and losing him. 'Only you have ever known if she would come.'

'That can't be so.'

But the old man was nowhere to be seen and the sea

hung in stillness, as if there had only ever been piles of stones and this space of grass.

No wind.

The red-legged crow, brân goesgoch, stood on one of the heaps. It had watched him work since the sky had brightened, the sun almost hidden behind grey cloud, day trying on winter clothing, whispering as it tried a few words in winter's voice before falling silent. A little cloud drifted across the face of the black sun, dimming the white shadows loitering at the base of the lighthouse. Just a little.

The space of grass waited for him to begin.

Honza reached out, trailing a finger over one of the heaps of stones, their faces cool and rough and solid.

'Do you think?'

The old man had been there, minutes before. The red-legged crow made no response and Honza, trying to remember the last few minutes, was sure he had spoken the other question out loud, not simply thought about pegs, string, guides to mark the centre and circumference, a shape to guide the shape to come. Yet the muscles of his throat felt unused—their memory was of silence, red bill and black wings, standing lost in thought.

The red-legged crow flew upwards, voice rough, a single word the lighthouse might once have spoken, or the waves. It might have been the old man's voice, close to the ear.

Honza knew the shape of the disk, without pegs and string, saw it in imagination, could see it on the ground instead of this rough grass trampled by the building and dismantling of the cairn.

What is it you see?

That might have been the tide, grey as wet stone. Or the bird. Or the breeze roosting on the curve of the mountaintop. It might have been the old man, or the clink of rock against rock as Honza selected the first stone and carried

the sun behind the mountain, a place of shadows, seeding another night, dusk turning over the cinders of the day. In the last of the light, the black sun appeared closer, hanging nearer to the lighthouse.

Honza lifted another stone, greying air chill against arms and face.

The stone fitted in quite well, mosaic taking form, disk an arc about one-third full, that arc turning about a centre point yet to be anchored, tufts of trampled grass filling in for now.

He straightened, back and legs tired after the day's work, fatigue part of the dusk and the coming night, like the ache in his shoulders and arms and hands, all this lifting and fitting into place, all this work. The chill air dried the sweat on his face. Honza took a few steps back

and leaned against the side of the cottage, jacket buttoned against the cold, another dawn walking down the path to the bay, opening its arms as the sun crossed the horizon, gilded light turning the island into a crucible, waves molten, pale stones of the disk becoming alabaster and opal, two-thirds complete, centre black in the sunrise, black as the sun fixed and unchanging over the lighthouse.

'Drink.' The old man held out a steaming cup, scent of

rosemary and nettle.

'There's not enough.' Honza blew, sipped, blew again. Tea hot against his throat, mug a coal in his hands. 'To complete the centre, I'll need another stone.'

Sunlight remade the bay, the long grass and the path to the water. Only the bird remained a shadow as it banked, settling nearby as the old man sipped from his own mug.

'I know somewhere,' he said.

Honza found it hard to look away from the sunrise. When he did

he walked carefully across the heath, ground underfoot vanishing each time the lighthouse beam swung away, darkness more complete with each passage, deep as the black sun, night moonless. The gap at the centre of the disk of stones was infinite, empty as the space between old moon and new. Frost on the air, nothing else: the sea had grown pensive as the wind fell away and the stars hid themselves behind masks of cloud. Only the lighthouse moved and that had not spoken in an age.

Honza took a breath.

On the next sweep, he looked inland. The cottages around the base of the mountain and along the road stood dark. No sign of the white cottage. No sign of the old man.

Honza took a breath as the beam orbited, casting his shadow like knucklebones but not pausing to read their omens, roving away and out to sea.

Blinking, Honza waited, breath held, unwilling to move in case this might change things, might mean the next sweep would show something different.

And when the beam did pass, he waited, unwilling to contradict the impression there had been someone at the bend in the road, watching. Not the old man but someone

waking.

I know where you can look for the last piece, the old man had said.

Honza stood beside the ruin. There was frost underfoot, sun yet to rise, the island nothing more than shapes and suggestions, few stars visible, the rest faded, day unformed. The cottage was a handful of metres away and that too looked uncertain and unfixed. Even in the light from above.

Honza did not look up.

It took a few minutes to find the right block, in the wall at the rear of the ruined abbey. Worm his fingers into the narrow seam, easing the block back and forth until it came free, revealed space enough to crawl into.

Just as the old man had described.

In the silence there was indecision and fear, the island smaller and darker with the block worked free than in the moments before. There was still time to put the stone back.

A chute, rough and uneven under hands and belly and knees. Slithering as much as crawling. Roof low, angle growing steeper and fear of slipping making the way harder. After a dozen metres, more, the passage levelled a little, taller as it descended into the earth, surface becoming uneven, less and less shaped by hand and mind, more crevice, an unfurling space through the rock, labyrinthine, perhaps without end, certainly no longer straight.

He lost track of distance. Time had meant nothing the instant the light from the entrance had snuffed out. The blackness grew cold, a physical presence across his face, eyes aching at its touch, skin prickling, each breath filled with it, the blackness soaking into vein and artery. Each scrape and shuffle forward made a brittle, scuttling sound, sound welling towards him along the passage, met by its echo rising from gut and bone and sinew, sounds merging, fumbling over each obstacle, each narrowing of the walls or dip in the pitch of the floor.

Muscles shook with the strain.

He kept moving.

No time, no duration. Only moving an arm, a hand, chest, waist, knee... No time, no past. Only an out-thrust of rock grazing knuckle, shoulder, surface beneath dipping, causing slip and hesitation. On this scale, muscles had always shaken, existed only in this instant of awareness and this awareness indistinguishable from rock, slip, cold, graze, breath-sound and breath-out, no different to darkness and its cold encircling.

Slumping. Inhale-exhale ragged. Pain. There were pains that could be unpicked from all else: the quality of pain in this muscle, the quality in that stubbed finger, the throb of a bruised cheek, a welt on the left shin, a scrape on the right ankle... Many pains and each great, small, different, asking for consideration, attention moving, next to another, finding itself fixed on the air, ice-honed, against forehead or palm, passing onto rock, a finger, a graze, a...

No time. So it could be it all happened in an instant as easily as any eternity. Breath slowing, less ragged, mouth and throat dry, teeth aching with the cold, muscles no longer quite so weak. Able to kneel, stoop, straighten as a hand exploring overhead found only empty space. Passage tall enough to walk upright.

So he walked.

Smell of cold, or rock and earth.
 Motion, foot in front of the other.
 Head ducked, in case. Hands out to balance, ward.
 Passage less steep. Still sloping.
 Downwards.

No sensation. Or dim sensation. Of cold and rock and sinew-muscle-bone. All dim. All black. Blank.
 Call that sleep.

Between that, walking. Slowly. Slower. Darkness unchanging. No time. Only earth, rock, balance, fatigue, breath, step, hesitation, forward, rock, narrowing, widening. Downwards.

Walking.

Sleep. Walking. Sleep.

Passage. Rock. Muscle. Bone. Pain (ache, graze, bruise, scrape, muscle, sinew). Sound (inside, outside: no distinction).

Fear. Knees thrust to floor. Scream. Screams. Go back go back goback goback gobackgobackgobackgobackgo— die will die will thirsthungerstarvedie will die you you

you will

you will

you

It passed. Left nothing behind.

A memory came: sunshine, grass, food, people. A picnic. Better than this, the memory suggested. Memory of a person, centre of attention, wanted, admired. An important person, the memory begged. Too important to be crawling, aching, cut, bruised, muscle bone rock earth darkness…

It passed. Left nothing behind.

Sisyphus climbed a hill and found a boulder at the top, which rolled down the hill. After, after shouldering it back to the foot of the slope, to just the spot he wanted, he struggled and heaved the boulder back up to the crest again. He waited, caught his breath, before rolling the rock all the way down again. The gods watched all this. They thought about punishing him, for reasons they could not name. But they did not, could not understand Sisyphus.

This passed.

Hunger, thirst: they passed.

The passage remained.
   It carefully walked itself, cautious in the darkness. Aware of rock, earth, the cold of this state between beginning and end, when there might be no end, only beginning. Aware of the uncertainty of balance, the weakness of step. They were at the forefront. Beneath, there was a familiarity to them that could be termed memory, although that suggested time, a past, a… someone to have experienced and remembered steps and fumbles and cold and breath and all the many other focal points of experience. And it suggested… someone consistent and continuous: a continuity of someone. Groping through the darkness for obstructions ahead. Taking a slow careful step. Another afterwards. Somewhere between beginning and end. Whatever that might mean. Earth rock step careful darkness fatigue ache: whatever they meant, the words   words what e ver   the   words   mean t   w hat e   v   e r

passed

gradually

absence growing black

gradually

black growing

grey

a dull crepuscular light hardly light at all but enough.
    Enough to remember seeing.
    Enough to see.

A cave. Just broader than arms outstretched. Tall enough to stand; roof close enough to touch. Sheen on the faces of the rocks almost enough to cast back a reflection.
    The passage sat, closed its eyes.

Oh, yes. Not 'passage'. Not exactly.

Honza gently explored the lines of his face. His fingers trembled. He might cry. If he could remember how. It had been so long. So very long.

There was nowhere for her to come from, there being only the cave; even the passage to here was no longer visible. Yet she approached, growing bigger, clearer with time's passing, time being a sequence of moments, each replacing the previous, and with each new instant's arrival, indistinguishable from the last, so she came closer. He thought of someone walking a long track that rose out of a dip. He thought of the painting Godfrey Howden had been so displeased with. She had not changed, not at all, although his memories of Prague and of her had faded, detail worn away by… time. It made him sad to know this and tears wormed between wrinkles and scars and old sagging flesh.

Don't be unhappy.

She knelt in front of him.

Don't cry, she said, taking his hand, her fingers cool and solid, her skin smooth and young. Don't cry over this. The heart remembers, remembers best. Your heart remembers.

I tried, he managed to say after a while, clutching her hand, shocked to see the shape of his fingers, the papery skin. I tried to listen, like she told me, the woman, in the restaurant, you remember.

Elnara, she nodded. But I wasn't there, Honza.

Oh… I tried to listen, he swore.

She said nothing, only held his hand.

It's too late now. He closed his eyes, seeing her too painful.

Why are you crying?

Her voice was gentle. He flinched even so.

Because… You know…

And if I don't? Tell me, Honza, please. And she squeezed his hand, tugging just a little until he looked at her, saw each part of her face, so ordinary, and saw her face, whole and in a single, sustained glance, as he had once at a picnic, many, many years ago. Seen like this, she was astonishing, filled with light, with beauty, with glorious energy.

He could not look away from her.

I… Lips dry. Voice a whisper. Of rain amongst branches and leaves. Of sea fret brushing against a shore. Of something from a great distance, unseen, unexpected, yet familiar once recognised anew. I… mourn… for…

The word escaped him.

He slipped his hand away and took one of hers in turn, captivated by the differences, joint and vein just beneath the skin, his skin a fallen leaf. For a few moments he expected his hands to blow away on her breath, autumn making way for winter's deep silence.

I never decided, you see.

To say so much a surprise and an effort. She waited and, at last, he continued.

I was told I followed. You. Your path.

No spit to swallow. Corner of the mouth gummed. A knee ached, one hip numbed from sitting on the cave floor. He would not let go of her hand.

But that…

Having begun it was hard to finish. Not rebuke, only… thusness. Turning breath into sound, he told her:

But that wasn't my choice.

Do you see? he asked later and she held his hand and leaned close because his voice was a whisper, less.

I followed you. And… and now…

No finishing this sentence. Tears and breath and contact, flesh and bone, warmth and presence.

Tell me, she urged.

And now… when it's too late, I know, I've decided, I've chosen. Only that. Only that.

Nothing more to say, he was sure, in this somewhere between beginning and end. This somewhere at the end.

Was it later, when she squeezed his hand, placed a palm against his cheek? Or was it in those instants, one merged into another, simply 'now', before breath and the sound it made had chance to fade and the cave fall silent?

It hardly mattered. The first star grew bright. And when she pointed, asked him to look, there was another star. Another and another, cave a suggestion in the night, an arc joining Orion and Cassiopeia, pointing towards Ursa Minor, Polaris spinning the arc about itself, Gemini back to Orion, to begin again, each connected, connections spreading, compounding, complex, dynamic. Living, yes, hard not to use the word, so: living and each living point drew him and touched him and welcomed him, although that sounded strange to say, except he found he was travelling from person to person, each person part of constellations unexpected, unnoticed when it had once seemed obvious that each person was as far apart as one star from another, alone in blackness, meaningless and alone, this assumption lying beneath each thought, each pencil stroke or dab of pigment, haunting him as he had stood and watched, or loved, or argued, or had been kind and caring: none of those things had changed the separation, the standing alone and watching; yet here were stars and constellations, their light peeling away the darkness as it peeled away the feeling of disconnection, encouraged him to look closer, see Imogen working on a canvas of her own, absorbed and yet on some level knowing he was near—and here, look here as Marie drew furious sketches, dropping a blunt pencil to the floor and snatching up another, and her passion was in him, shared and exchanged in some way and in some way it was the same with Jaromír lost in thought over a photograph, and with Elnara, with the baker… an empathy, a… no framing it in words, too clumsy, too much time because he moved so fast, a star beam, a mote following alignments, connective points: the baker in his van, to Elnara praying, to Jaromír in reverie to… to Godfrey Howden striding along a street in New York, thought leaping to thought, leaping to Rose Greer, mixing herbs in her laboratory, to Karel, screwing up a sheet of paper and beginning another poem: each one part of this as he was, part of something complex, subtle, ridiculously obvious now he was open to it, as it opened to him, guided him to kneel beside a gently bubbling iron pot, the bells of a temple sounding in the near distance, the woman leaning forward to stir the pot, singing a snippet of song beneath her breath and he sang it too and although he did not know Japanese he knew the meaning of the song and he held out his hand to each person passing by, Cairo busy at this time of day, surely someone willing to spare something and the tears would not stop, the sorrow touching her as she walked and he walked beside her along the dusty track, African sun a weight to be balanced as carefully as the ewer she carried on her head, graceful in a way that made him want to cry again although she smiled and he smiled, for a moment, before going on to the next rosary bead, church silent but for the man's voice, the Andes watching over the town as he watched over his prayers, smiling a little at simple graces, too commonplace to be noticed most days but today... today... there were so many, each leading on: past a man with alabaster white hair as pale as his tall wife's skin, couple standing side by side on a high hilltop watching the road meandering closer, a figure on the road approaching, another star in this supremely vast, elegantly simple constellation where no point was ever more than an arm length away, or less, much less, and he took her hand as she came closer along the road, in this cave that breathed and wept and shone with the light of countless, countless stars.

It lay beside him. The stone. The last piece.

There was no end to the tunnel, the stone pushed in front of him upslope a few centimetres at a time. Darkness stretched distances, asked over and over how much he wanted to return to the surface, how significant this hunk of the rock was. He took no notice, crawled another few centimetres, another few, until there was no denying the smell of brine, the change in the air. Darkness remained. It was not night.

Vast. Filling a quarter of the sky, weaving a white corona around each shadow, halos overlapping, as if there were many, each in a different position above the lighthouse. Only one, though. Only one back sun.

His hands were black, skin smokey, pitch as the shadows charged with the black sun's pulse. The stone collected reflections in the shallow hollow at its centre, presenting a face of shades of crimson and scarlet.

His face red.

Hands and arms black.

Feet… torso…

Black.

Red.

Red and black.

Surf hissed, tide anxious as he moved, rock by rock, across the disk and lowered the stone into the space at the centre.

Waves became still.

The black sun lay close to the eastern horizon, searching for its reflection in the disk of stones, the last stone at their centre itself a circle facing towards the black sun.

Breeze became still. The grass no longer hissed.

He waited, not sure what might happen. The black sun brushed against the sea, not setting but fading, a fog dissipating, dusk giving way to moonrise, light soft honied gold, a light that could never be captured or recreated, could only exist in moments such as this.

The black sun dwindled, grew too faint to see. Where it had stood, a single star shone.

Coming closer.

He managed to look away long enough to take the first step, had to keep watching after that, slipping and stumbling but not falling as he clambered down to the beach, watching the star come closer over the sea, light unfolding to reveal its centre.

There were tears. Breath hitching, he rubbed away the tears. They did not stop and he almost retreated up the beach, the joy too much.

He held out his hands. Black skin. Red. Held out his hands towards her as she approached over the sea, awed into stillness as she stepped onto the sand.

She was beautiful. Not flawless, nor perfect, not exactly that. But beautiful. There was something of himself in her face, around the eyes, a distant reflection or family resemblance many times removed. He smiled, like the sea, awed into stillness and unable to do anything but smile, hands still held out towards her.

Her. The star from the sea.

Who are you?

The question was asked. Out loud; in mind—the difference was irrelevant.

She took his hands.

You know me, she replied, in dreams you've seen me, in dreams I've watched you. You know me.

And she told him her name, which was a sound and a simple, encompassing gesture and the colour of a particular moment, repeated but oft-times overlooked: these things and many other subtle constellations of meaning.

He did not understand and she told him it did not matter.

Look—

She took his hand and drew him to look away from her, towards the lighthouse.

The foundations remained, roots grown through them, out, fixed deep in the island: a tree, as tall as the lighthouse had been, taller, branches in leaf, in bud, heavy with ripe fruit.

Who are you? he asked again.

You know, she told him, enfolding him in a close and tender embrace.

Anima, he thought, as if that explained everything.

When she opened her arms, she was alone on the beach.

Dew collected in the stone at the centre of the disk, enough for her to see her reflection in the water.

Will he return? the old man asked, building a fire.

He's here. She washed herself in the dew. He never went away.

And she sat beside the fire, drying herself. The heat worked through flesh to what lay beneath.

Honza turned over his hands, skin ruddied by the fireglow, no longer black, no longer red. He leaned forward and gathered the old man's hands in his own. And saw himself, leaning over to take his hands, heard his voice with the old man's ears as he heard it with his own, felt his hands as if he clasped himself.

Three becomes two and from the two, one. Yet from one comes two, and from that three, out of which many. Which become three, are two, are one, are…

It felt better that there were two, for now two, companions crossing the heath to the foot of the tree.

Would you choose one, he asked the old man, choose a branch?

It's your choice.

Yes. This is my choice. Please?

The old man chose a branch. It did not break but came away at their touch, a stout limb, a keel curved into a prow, stern and rudder, mast an axis from which to plot a course, sail billowing as the wind rose, as Honza tacked around the headland, westward, the old man's voice in his ear, voice becoming bow wake and wave and the thrum of wind and sail. Westwards, following the sun's track until the boat grew small with distance, until, for a moment or an eternity, it made no difference, until there were two suns, one vanishing beneath the western horizon as the other rose in the east, people coming out of their cottages, to tend farm animals, draw water, push fishing boats out into the bay, the painter inspired by the early morning light to draw and paint, wondering where the young man had gone, the one who had visited yesterday and must have taken a boat back to the mainland in the late afternoon.

And the lighthouse, white tower unmissable on the rise above the sea, emitted a single bell-like note before it fell silent in the winter sunshine.

AFTERWARDS

WHEN IT BECAME obvious the young artist had not returned to the mainland, a search was made of the island as well as the sea and down the coast along the path of the tides. With neither body nor word of his whereabouts, it was assumed he was lost. However, during the first months of the Second World War, stories began to circulate that he had been a spy. It was said he lit signal fires to attract submarines; that there was a radio transmitter hidden beneath the ruined abbey. An alleged witness circulated a bizarre tale of seeing the young man walking on the sea in the moonlight. Curiously, it was this story that gained greatest currency in the 1950s, becoming linked to both rumours of secret technological breakthroughs and with flying saucers. By the 1960s, the tale had grown more elaborate and it was often repeated, in books and magazines, that the missing artist was an experimenter who had tapped into mysterious earth energies and developed the power to cross dimensions. In the early 1970s, the earnest and the curious went to the island, hoping to find a clue, or make a sighting of some kind. Ghost, ufonaut, magician: the missing man was all that and more.

Another decade brought another story: the artist had been abducted by aliens. And, in the 1990s, it was claimed the whole thing was a hoax contrived by intelligence agencies to hide activities elsewhere.

By the beginning of the new century, the story of the vanished artist had become a mirror reflecting the face of whoever told it, not one story any longer but many. With the slow-drip of the Howden papers—the so-called *Lost Book of Theseus*—one or two researchers claimed Godfrey Howden had known the vanished man; there was certainly a window in Howden's life when he could have gone to Prague, might have met a certain artist who seemed to drop out of history on the cusp of the Second World War, and whose work had recently attracted re-evaluation and rising auction prices. There was a very romantic story, apparently corroborated in a few diary entries made by friends and colleagues at the time, that this artist had gone in search of the young woman who had been his muse. There was no mention of such a woman in official records and if there is more in unofficial sources, it has yet to come to light.

There seems no knowing the truth behind the missing artist's many interconnected tales. Not unless he appears to give his own testimony. Which must be unlikely. Even his name is uncertain. The Czech artist mentioned in diaries and letters went by a *nom d'art*—there are no records of his real name or his birth, any more than there are of his death. 'Honza Pernath' is a convenience, a cypher. A rebus. Yes, that's the word.

A rebus.

Lightning Source UK Ltd.
Milton Keynes UK
UKHW011303011022
409759UK00002B/27